BLOOD BOUND BOOKS

Presents

SEASONS IN THE ABYSS

EDITED BY JACK BURTON

 Cover art by Gary McCluskey.

Visit us on the web at:
www.bloodboundbooks.net

Available now from Blood Bound Books:

Night Terrors: An Anthology of Horror
Unspeakable: A New Breed of Terror

Coming Soon:

D.O.A.: Extreme Horror Collection
Rock is Dead: Dark Tales Inspired by Music
Steamy Screams: Erotic Horror Anthology

The Blood Bound Staff:

Marc Ciccarone
Joe Spagnola
Theresa Dillon
Karen Fierro

And
Special thanks to Richard Ciccarone

WINTER

SPRING

SUMMER

FALL

WINTER

Staving Off the Thaw

Gef Fox

At its best, the snow fort's walls reached just over Nicky's head. Now though, the walls barely made it to his waist. The thaw had come early.

"It's not fair," he said.

"It wasn't going to last forever," his brother Theo replied.

They sat beside each other inside the snow fort in the backyard. Small blades of grass peaked out from the trodden snow. An ocean of green surrounded them outside the fort's crumbling walls. The weatherman on TV promised nothing but sunshine and freezing temperatures. He lied. The sun hid behind gray clouds and the thermometer read five degrees above freezing. The snow fort Nicky had built for his big brother was the last of the snow in the valley.

Theo would have to leave soon.

"I don't want you to go," Nicky said.

Theo shrugged. "I don't want to go either. I've had fun with you, but rules are rules."

"The rules are stupid." They'd been over it before, so Nicky didn't bother arguing it further. The agreement was that Theo could visit during the winter for as long as the fort lasted.

At their backs was the rear entrance to the fort—a bottomed-out pickle barrel tipped on its side. Each evening, Theo said goodnight to Nicky and crawled through the barrel and disappeared until the next day. Nicky tried to follow him a couple times, but he only ended up on the other side of the barrel. Wherever Theo went, Nicky wasn't allowed to go. Maybe it was Heaven, but Theo never said and Nicky was afraid to ask.

"I'll get more snow. You can keep coming back if I find more snow."

"But there's no more snow. This is it."

Theo reached over and scraped at one of the walls. The snow fell away in small clumps.

"Don't!" Nicky grabbed at Theo's arm. "There's still snow up on the hills. I'll walk up with the sled and bring more down."

It was almost a mile through the hayfields and woods at the foot of the hills across the road. From there, it was a steep climb through more trees. Only the top third of the hills showed signs of snow.

"Nicky, it's too far. Here ..." Theo reached into their war chest—a tin Tasmanian Devil lunch box—and grabbed the pack of Playboy playing cards Nicky had snuck out of their father's desk. "... Let's play some cards for a bit. I'll let you win this time."

"I can't *not* do anything." Nicky stood up and looked down at his big brother. "I'm getting more snow. I'm going to keep you alive."

"But I'm not alive."

Nicky stormed off.

By the time he was halfway across the hayfield with sled in hand, he was already sweating, so he stuffed his mittens in his pockets. He hurried his way through the trees and trudged up the hill until he came upon the first patches of snow. Like the edges of the snow fort, the snow was rotten and loose like gravel—but this snow was dirty with flecks of tree bark and moss. In his haste, Nicky had forgotten to bring a shovel or bucket, so he used his bare hands to scoop the snow into the sled. When his hands got cold and clammy from handling it, he put his mittens back on and kept scooping even after they became saturated.

He only had what amounted to a few shovelfuls when he heard the rain start. He looked up and a drop struck his right eye. He winced and wiped it away.

A trepid chant of *no-no-no* poured from his mouth as he descended the hill. In the fields, he felt the full force of the rain—no longer a sprinkling, the drops fell heavy and straight down. When Nicky started to run, the sled tipped to one side and the snow spilled into the still-matted grass. He knelt down and scooped up what he could; as he worked, he heard his labored breath turn to heavy sobs. The rain continued to beat down on his sodden snow cap.

"It's not fair!"

He looked down at what little snow he had salvaged. It was useless. There wasn't enough. He looked across the fields towards home. He couldn't see the fort in the backyard, but the worst had entered his mind. As he ran back, screaming his big brother's name, Nicky prayed he was still there. He thought about the afternoons after school with Theo, laughing about how lame the teachers were, and Theo teasing him about the homework he had to do; and on the weekends the snowball fights they had and the toy soldiers and card games. They never fought, not now or ever again. It was the perfect winter and it wasn't fair that Theo had to die. Nicky wished he could go to Heaven with his brother and build a snow fort there.

Nicky rounded the corner of the house. Theo wasn't there. He raced to remnants of the fort and fell to his knees calling Theo's name through the barrel. No answer came. He yelled out for Theo to come back, then he noticed one of the playing cards inside the barrel. It was the extra one with the rules for poker on it that they never used. On the back, Theo had written a final note to Nicky.

Rules are rules.

The Night of the Wolf

Pete Mesling

Her hands worked the needle back and forth through the fibrous pattern as though she were stitching a world into being. She was dexterous when she wanted to be, nimble and sure. But she'd been chopping her own wood for coming on two decades, so she also knew the value of brute force.

A smile played on her lips, and thinking about it made her smile even more. There'd been a time when Dorothy Madigan doubted so much as a smirk would ever find its way onto her face again. Amazing what the mind is able to put aside over time. Time's a healer, sure enough.

But healing is not the same as preventing, and, even as the years wipe away past trials, they carry us ever closer to the next great catastrophe. If Dorothy's spirit had been only as hard and implacable as the rounds of old wood she quartered for winter burning, she would have folded under the weight of such knowledge. A future as black as her past was a grim prospect, but she was ready for the fuckers this time.

Storm clouds had sneaked up on her while she plied her needle. They peeked in through the narrow window she counted on for light. Intrusive bastards, she thought. Hadn't anyone told them it's rude to sneak up on an old woman? Her smile broke into a chuckle. Spittle flew from between her teeth, slicking the embroidery in her lap.

The time had come. Rising up out of her old rocker was a good piece of work, but she got the job done without dropping her needlework or pricking a finger. The chair groaned with relief. Her daddy always used to call her ample-bosomed, but hell and damn if her ass hadn't caught up with her chest and then some. Aging was one of time's lesser miracles.

She deposited her half-finished needlepoint in a drawer and shuffled to the rear of the cabin. At the far end of a short hall stood an ancient trunk. To the left was the bedroom, to the right a door leading out back. Dorothy swept a hand across the oily wooden surface of the trunk before lifting the lid and propping it open with a stick she left inside for that very purpose. She quickly disrobed, leaving her cotton dress and underclothes in a heap, and reached into the trunk with both hands.

It felt alive between her fingers, not like a mangy old pelt. Tonight they would come padding through the new fallen snow again, she thought, unfolding the wolf skin, which seemed to ripple as she let it out. This time she would not cower, would not watch them snatch her husband and rip him apart, feast on him. Tonight things would be different. Not much had changed since the night her life was cleaved in two, but one thing had. The spirit of Hobbamock had sung to her in a dream, and she followed him into the mist, learning his ways of protection and justice, amid the trees and the animals.

She only had to lay one corner of the pelt on her shoulder and it crawled across her back to tighten itself. The hood of ears and muzzle pressed itself onto her head and she was forced into a stoop. A smell came on her like decaying flowers. She unlatched the door, pushed it open with her shoulder, and loped into the chill dusk, howling a plaintive but satisfied note. They were just beyond the ridge now. Their stink betrayed them. This night, the element of surprise was hers.

The Grotto

Louise Broadbent

"Can't I go into Game while you take Sal to see Father Christmas?"

"No."

"Why not?"

"Because we're spending some time as a family and I don't want to lose you in this crowd. Besides, you've wasted enough money on those stupid computer games."

"They're not stupid."

"Look, Fred, your sister wants to go, and we're all going together. OK?"

"This is stupid. It's just for stupid little kids who—"

"OK?"

Fred shrugged.

"Right then."

Fred leaned to the side to search for Santa's Grotto at the front of the long line. It tormented him with its tacky, fake, Americanized jollity. Sally gibbered about Santa and pointy elves and the big, pretty tree.

"It's not *Santa*, it's Father Christmas, idiot."

"Don't call your sister an idiot."

Sally sneaked her head behind her mum's back and stuck her tongue out at him. Fred scoffed and looked away towards the tree. There were moving gnomes on it, turning their heads to peer at the crowd.

The line edged forward.

"Who thinks gnomes are a good Christmas tree decoration?"

"I don't know."

"They're freaking me out."

"You always say that. Last year you said you didn't like the way the penguins moved," his mother replied. "You're not getting out of this."

"They move weird."

"I don't care, Fred."

"But these gnomes...They're...There's something off about them. Almost sinister."

"Oh shut up, Frederick. You're giving me a headache."

Sally started to squeal along with *Santa Claus is Coming to Town*.

Fred shook his head and tried to hum *I Believe in Father Christmas* but kept losing it in the American song. He stepped out of line to see how far it was now. He frowned. One of the gnomes in the tree caught his eye. Was it looking at him?

"Mum."

"What now?"

"Where are the people coming out of the grotto?"

"How should I know?"

"I can't see anyone coming out," Fred said.

"Well, the exit is probably hidden from view. It'll be on the other side of the tree."

"But that's where Debenhams is."

"Well, maybe you go straight into the shop. You probably end up in the toys section."

Fred shook his head.

"Let's try to get *in* first, shall we?"

"Something's not right, mum."

"Oh for goodness' sake, Fred, stop trying to wind me up."

"I'm not, mum. That gnome keeps looking at me."

"It's looking at everyone. What's the matter with you?"

Fred shook his head, again. That gnome's eyes were fixed on him. Its head cocked to one side as a grin slithered over its face.

The line edged forward.

"Mum, I don't like this."

"Oh just stop it, will you? You're ruining it for your sister."

"But that gnome. Look at it."

As she turned to look at the gnome, it started moving like all the others, only its eyes still seemed pinned on Fred. Then it winked at him.

"How would you like to go next, eh?" a voice said.

Fred gasped at the elf crouching by Sally.

"Oh, but all those people were here before us."

Fred stared at the elf. Were those ears real?

"Yes, but, Santa says that this little girl's the sweetest and he wants her next." The elf grinned at Fred. Pointy little teeth were waiting in rows behind its lips.

Sally hopped like a vulture. "Please, mummy. I want to see Santa. Pleeeaaase."

"No!" The shout leapt from Fred's throat. A few people ahead of them turned to stare at him.

"Oh, Fred, don't be so stroppy. All right Sal, we can go next, as long as the, er, lady? says it's OK."

The elf's grin grew. It gripped Fred's arm and pushed him towards the grotto, behind his mum and baby sister. "The American name is more appropriate," it whispered in his ear, ignoring his struggling. "You'll see when you meet the real—"it pushed him inside, "—Santa *Claws*."

Melting Snow

Charles Day

Jake peered out his bedroom window, as he had so many mornings this past week, watching the snow fall. Truth be told, staring out the window was more than a morning ritual. It filled most of his days since…

He shook the unpleasant memory from his aching head and closed his eyes. He re-opened them and focused again on the grey sky. The gently floating flurries, however, did nothing to alleviate the throbbing pain in his head. The pain had gotten worse over the course of the week. He rubbed his temples, feeling hypnotized by the piling blankets of snow.

Boom, boom, boom, his head continued pulsing and the snow kept falling.

He blinked, slowly coming out of the daze and focused on his yard, just to the left of where his shed was located, to a small area of dirt. The patch was void of the white powder which fell from the sky. On either side of the dirt, small piles of snow began rising, but nothing touched that patch of dirt.

Jake's heart caught in his throat. "What the Fuck?" Jake spoke to the empty room. He suddenly wished someone was there to sit with him. But there was no one. There hadn't been any one in the house since his wife left him a year ago, taking their two year old and only child with her.

He leaned closer to the window. The pulsing in his head grew louder. A part of him wanted her to come back, but it was better she was gone. She cheated on him with another man and she tried to keep the love affair a secret. That was until he came home one day and found her straddling the bastard on his living room sofa.

But that's all over with now. I made sure.

"So… it can't be," Jake whispered, grabbing his coat as he ran downstairs towards the back door.

Before he could open the door, his cell phone rang. Frustrated he opened the phone. "Yes, what is it Marge?"

His wife, the one person he didn't want to converse with at

this moment answered. “I know you’re up to something Jake, I just know it. I can’t pin you to it, but I’ll be dammed if you didn’t say or do something to Sam. I haven’t heard from him for five days.”

The sound of her boyfriend’s name sent the pounding in his head into overdrive. It felt like drums were being played inside his skull.

“I don’t want to hear it, Marge. I’m far from worrying about some guy screwing you and then leaving ya,” Jake spoke sarcastically, his hand still on the back door handle.

“He didn’t leave me!” She shouted. “I bet you threatened him to stay away.”

Her voice was rising with emotions and the pitch was hurting his head. Jake closed his eyes, trying to ignore the sound while Marge continued squawking about how Sam was not someone to mess with.

“He might be staying away for now. But it’s only because he’s planning a way at getting back at you.”

“Sure,” Jake said, opening the door and stepping outside. He knew Sam wasn’t planning anything.

Jake stepped off his wooden deck, almost tumbling as his work boots sunk into a mush of white. He balanced himself to keep from falling as he wiped the wind driven snow from his eyes with one hand.

He could barely hear her through the cell phone over the howling wind. “You don’t know what he’s capable of. He came from way down south Jake, where they practice that hoodoo stuff and all. Said his family taught him well.”

“Sorry, Marge, gotta go. Hope he comes back to ya.” He hung up the phone and continued to the rectangular patch of dirt. Each step brought more pain to his aching skull. Pounding, pounding away, like drums…

Like voodoo drums, he thought, remembering Marge’s words.”

“That’s bullshit!” he shouted over the wind and the pounding.

Within two more steps, he stood over the snow free patch of dirt. The area was roughly 6 ft long and 4 feet wide. And every inch was free of snow. Jake bent down and touched the dirt still not believing what he was seeing. The warmth of the dead grass and soil sent him back on his rear.

He jumped up instantly, brushing the cold ground from the back of his pants. Jake began pacing back and forth. My ex is trying to scare me, telling me that her lover is into voodoo or hoodoo or Scooby-doo, whatever. All I know is she's a lying cheat, and…

To the left of the dirt, the doors of the shed swung open from a gust of fierce, snow driven wind. Jake had a clear view into the shed and all its tools hanging from the wooden racks inside. However, only one caught his eye: the shovel.

"Jesus, what's going on?" Jake screamed out loud. He raced to the shed and grabbed the shovel as if it was calling to him. He stepped back into the cold and poised the shovel over the ground.

What if Marge were right? Her lover was part of some voodoo cult, he thought gripping the shovel. The same shovel he used to dig the hole beneath the patch of dirt that refused the touch of snow. The same shovel that reassured Jake that there was no way Sam could do anything to him.

Jake lifted the shovel in mid air and sent the spade straight into the mound of dirt. The pounding drums crescendoed to the point where Jake felt his ear drums would burst. Jake threw away a huge mound of dirt, then another. He dropped the shovel and fell to his knees to brush away the remaining dirt. He placed his palms on the dirt and suddenly the pounding in his head stopped. Everything seemed to end and he could breathe properly.

I'm being crazy, Jake laughed into the cold air. *Just the stress of it all. I shouldn't feel bad though. He's the one who…*

Suddenly the frozen hand of the man he had drugged, murdered and buried in his backyard, reached out from the earth and grabbed him by the throat.

"Help! Holy shit, help me!" Jake managed to squeak out before the muscular hand cut off his air and began pulling him into the fresh dirt.

By night fall, Jake's backyard was covered in snow. The whole backyard. Leaving no trace of the bodies buried beneath.

Trapped Under Ice

Robert Essig

Even after Ryan threw the large boulder, indicating the structural integrity of the ice, Paul's first steps were apprehensive.

"Are you sure about this?" asked Paul, his fifteen-year-old inhibitions setting in.

"Do it every year," replied Ryan.

It was hard to tell where the lake's shore ended being that the snow created a white landscape that could hide anything, but Ryan knew his way around quite well, having grown up in North Dakota, unlike Paul who hailed from California.

Every time they reached the boulder, Ryan would heft it up and throw it as far as he could to make sure the ice was solid enough to walk on.

"We're just about at the center of the lake," said Ryan.

It wasn't as much of a spectacle as Paul thought walking on a frozen lake would be.

"What's so special about the lake?" asked Paul.

"Fish live in the freezing water, but they swim at the bottom. If we clear away some of the snow and look real hard, maybe we can see one."

Paul shrugged, "Okay."

They fell to their knees and swept the snow away with gloved hands until crystalline ice was visible. Wind blew dropping stalactites from frozen trees and the occasional tuft of snow from frozen branches.

"I don't see anything," said Paul.

"The light attracts them. Give it time."

Paul couldn't figure out just what the thrill in watching half frozen fish was, but he went along with the plan just the same.

"I brought something to pass the time," said Ryan as he produced a half a pack of cigarettes. "Took 'em from my father. Wanna try one?"

Paul regarded the cigarette about as warily as he did the ice, but he took it nonetheless and choked heartily on the first drag as the smoke burned his lungs.

Ryan laughed as he took a drag like a life-long smoker. "You'll get used to it."

"Tastes like shit," said Paul as he exaggeratedly tapped his ash on the exposed plot of ice where no fish dared swim. He watched the ash fall, and saw the first glimmer of something. "I see one!"

"Oh, yeah?" Ryan looked closer.

Both teens peered into the dark void silently waiting for a glimpse, and then a shape formed, rising from the depths, larger than any fish they had ever seen in a lake.

"What the—" said Ryan.

Then a face became clear, the eyes opaque, mouth opening and closing as it ascended, wrinkled palms flat on the underbelly of the ice. It happened so slow and gruesomely graceful that both Paul and Ryan were locked in shock, hearts beating double-time.

An eerie old man stared at them from beneath the ice. He balled his fist and pounded, hardly making a sound yet causing the boys to jump back as if the man would break through and pull them under.

"Shit!" said Paul. "What's wrong with him?"

"He must have fallen in!" yelled Ryan. "We gotta get him out!"

"But—" Paul started, considering the fact that no one would be able to survive in such frigid conditions, not to mention the dead eyes the old man stared at them with.

Before Paul could further protest, Ryan hauled the boulder above his head and threw it down with far more force than he had previously while checking the stability of the ice. This time cracks formed that stretched from the boulder's point of impact in several directions.

"What are you doing?" yelled Paul. "You're going to drown us!"

"He needs help. He's gonna die under there if we don't get him out."

Ryan removed the rock, pulling broken shards of ice away in a panic, Paul standing behind him motionless. Paul knew something was terribly wrong, knew there was no way the man could have fallen in the lake. He looked at the flawless blanket of snow from one end of the lake to the other. There were no signs of a disturbance.

"We should leave, Ryan."

Ryan looked to Paul. "Leave? Are you crazy? We have to help this man. You can live with this on your conscience? You can leave without at least trying to help?"

Ryan continued pulling larger pieces of ice away, the cracks beneath his feet growing as he did so.

"He can't be alive, Ryan. Don't you see? Something's wrong here."

"He's moving, Paul! I can see that. I don't know what's wro—"

A blue hand broke through the ice grabbing Ryan's wrist and violently yanking his arm into the frozen lake. Ryan screamed as he tried desperately to pull his arm from the grip of the old man.

"Help!" screamed Ryan. "Paul, help me!"

Paul ran to his friend. There was an ear piercing scream as Paul yanked Ryan free, both of them falling backwards onto the cracked ice. There was blood, but in the panicked moment Paul couldn't tell from where the blood came. He could hear the ice cracking beneath their bulk and knew they had to get to the lake's edge before they fell into the icy water.

"C'mon, Ryan!" Paul grabbed his friend hauling him onto his feet. Ryan cried, pain shocking the stub where his arm had been. Just before they made their way from the cracked ice, Paul saw the old grizzled man beneath, his milky eyes glaring at them. In his mouth was Ryan's arm. Paul shivered at the sight, then helped his friend off the ice, the whole time wondering if the old man beneath was hoping they would hit a weak spot in the ice and fall through.

A Hungry December

Michael R. Colangelo

Wheeler and I were walking with little destination in mind.

It was cold and we were both hungry and tired. We had nothing to eat but the bucket of paste we'd brought along on the job.

Wheeler was talking, as always.

"...and you don't see fucking Laura out here with us, do you?"

He was always on her case about one thing or another. He was always complaining about Laura. He was always complaining. So much so that nothing he said mattered much, anymore.

So we were just walking and barely working.

In hindsight, I might have said we were looking for a better place to put up the rest of the fliers, but that wouldn't be the truth.

We were just trudging in a general direction. We were just wasting away the afternoon.

But Wheeler has little to do with this, and this has everything to do with me.

My ancestors were Dutch immigrants. They were some of the first to cross the ocean. We've even got a turnpike named after us somewhere in south Pennsylvania.

And with all the cold and starving that Wheeler and Laura and I have been up against lately, I've been thinking a lot about my roots.

Not in the way that Wheeler's always going on about how he wished he never moved here from the East Coast, but in the way that those early pioneers must have felt about it.

The cold, the hunger and the isolation must have been crushing at times. Way worse off than we are now—maybe.

When I start thinking about that stuff, I start thinking about how they managed it, too.

The conclusion I draw is always the same.

The solution is static.

But I didn't have time to reach any conclusions that afternoon, because Wheeler punched me in the shoulder blade as hard as he could. The blow jarred me from my old thoughts about ancient kin.

"Look there, John." He pointed across a six-lane freeway to a supermarket complex on the other side. "We could go check it out."

What he meant was that he wanted to go dumpster diving. These places threw out perfectly good food all of the time. I knew that Wheeler didn't actually give a shit about eating. What he wanted to do was return to the squat with a bounty in his arms, like some Viking prince returning to his keep after a hearty pillaging.

Also, I had no idea why he thought it was a good idea to run across the highway.

But arguing with Wheeler was like banging your head against the sidewalk until your skull shattered and your brains leaked out until there was nothing left inside of it.

So I shrugged and said, "What the fuck, Wheeler, let's go get something to eat, then.

Wheeler went first. He handed me the paste bucket and went snaking beneath the chain link fence separating us from the asphalt highway.

Then he made a run for it.

There were hints of carnage as he zigzagged across the freeway. The sounds of screeching brakes and blaring horns continually threatened to metamorphose into more tragic sounds. But Wheeler kept his eyes on the other side, and soon I could see him safe and wiggling beneath the fence on the opposite side of the roadway.

It was my turn next, so I ditched the bucket and stepped into traffic.

I'm pretty sure I had my epiphany at that moment, as tons of speeding, crushing metal and glass threatened to end it all from every side of me.

No pioneer ever had to risk their life running across a highway to pick through the garbage on the other side.

I made it, somehow. When I surfaced in the parking lot, Wheeler greeted me laughing.

He was a fucking idiot. Wheeler was little more than a mindless automaton that was driven by whatever compelled him—which was mostly Laura. Food and shelter and safety mattered not.

I realized I was allowing myself to be led by some blind idiot god-child. My ancestors would be disappointed to say the least. But now I knew what they would do to remedy the problem.

We dug through the garbage.

The sun was setting, so we took our treasures and headed back to the squat. Laura was passed out on the couch when we got there, and Wheeler lay down beside her, leaving me to prepare our meal.

We'd gotten pretty lucky with the place we were staying at. The apartment had a little kitchenette and there was still a knife and a big, industrial kitchen meat tenderizer in the island drawers. The bathtub in the bathroom was in pretty good shape, too.

As I moved toward the couch, I envisioned my ancestors, snowed in and starving, choosing the weakest of the lot.

That was Wheeler, and Laura was passed out anyway.

So what would they do? Stun them first, probably.

Wheeler's only reaction when I hit him with the tenderizer was a bit of flutter around his eyes and beneath his eyelids.

What next?

I didn't have a slaughter hook, but the bathtub would do for the bleed out. I dragged him there and worked quickly.

When I was done with him, Laura was next. Suddenly, there were days of food available to me. It would last even longer if I could get my hands on some ice.

I ate them raw.

It was historically inaccurate, perhaps, but I felt they tasted better that way.

Halted Progress

Ben McElroy

Even at the age of eighty, Martin still indulged his inner child on occasion. Today, for example, he and his great-grandnephew, Sean, planned to construct a snowman after lunch. For now, though, they fiddled with an old pair of binoculars.

"What's that, Uncle Marty?" Sean asked while using the device.

"What's what, Sean?" Martin asked.

"That dark spot in the sky over there."

Martin looked out to where Sean's small finger pointed. Then he said, "Looks like another storm's coming our way. Guess we should go build that snowman now instead of waiting until later."

Sean dropped the binoculars and ran over to the mud room, where he donned his winter gear. With a smile, Martin sauntered over to the boy. Once there, he put on his own coat, boots, gloves and scarf.

Soon, Martin and Sean crossed the street to a snow-covered cornfield that was part of Martin's nephew's farm.

"So how big would you like to make Frosty?" Martin asked.

Sean grinned and said, "Taller than if I stood on your shoulders."

"Great. You start rolling the bottom half of the body, and I'll supervise to be sure you're doin' an okay job of it."

Sean set about his task with a gusto reserved only for the very young. A gust of frigid wind blew across the field, Martin shivered and sighed. Remembering the storm cloud Sean pointed out earlier, Martin looked up at the sky. His breath hitched. The dark cloud now hovered over the entire western horizon. But it didn't look so much like a cloud anymore. It now resembled an immense black shroud.

Just then, snow started to fall much to Sean's delight, judging by the boy's high pitched giggles. Martin glanced over at him. Sean had completed all but the snowman's head.

"Sean, why don't we head on inside? That storm looks like a whopper," Martin said.

"But Uncle Marty," Sean said.

"I really think we ought to hustle ourselves into the house."

"I'm almost done though."

"There's no time, boy. Get moving."

Martin peered up at the inky blackness overhead. It had advanced a great distance; it now loomed directly above them. Martin's limbs began to tremble but not from the cold. He blinked his eyes to be sure he actually saw what he thought he had seen.

The snowflakes closest to the approaching dark mass had halted in mid-fall. A cardinal had also been suspended twenty feet in the air. As Martin observed this eerie phenomenon, he witnessed the snowflakes, the bird, the trees, and everything else vanish as the darkness overtook the cornfield.

"Run, Sean, run," Martin said.

The boy did just that. Unfortunately, Martin experienced limited mobility due to the arthritis in his knees. Still, he marched through the snow as best he could.

At that very moment, Sandy, Sean's golden retriever, came bounding over to Martin. The canine barked and jumped and circled the old man. Then she ran behind him, toward the towering wall of shadows.

Sandy must've sensed something amiss, for she growled and started to turn back to run toward Martin. But the blackness was quicker.

The dog's hindquarters became paralyzed. Whimpering, she clawed at the frozen ground in front of her. With her head thrust forward and her eyes wide and wild, Sandy screeched as if in extreme agony.

Martin's lower jaw quivered. Tears filled his eyes at the sight before him. He turned to check on Sean's progress. The boy must've made it into the house, for there was no sign of him.

Taking a deep breath, Martin waited for the inevitable. He couldn't outrun whatever this darkness was. He had no choice but to stand his ground and accept whatever was about to happen to him. He shuffled around until he faced the unstoppable force. Keeping his eyes open, he mouthed a silent prayer.

Seconds later, the mass was upon him. Indescribable creatures and even a few malformed humans lurked within the shadows.

Then Martin felt his entire body freeze up. There was no pain. Martin used his final thought to hope that his family would be spared this horrific fate; perhaps he was the intended victim and not them.

In the very next instant, Martin was simply gone.

The Red Thing in the Snow

Adrian Ludens

The red thing in the snow got into his head.

Gabriel Dawson stood at the window and gazed out at the white expanse of strange formations and mysterious outcroppings that winter had transformed his back yard into. Naked shrubs hunched like skeletal hens nesting in defiance of the bitter wind. Clouds of snowflakes twisted and capered in the frigid air like Nordic demons on holiday.

And there was the red thing in the snow to consider.

Gabe squinted and tried to identify the object that seemed to nestle in the ever-shifting white banks. A piece of trash? A child's red mitten or half-hidden scarf? Gabe couldn't quite decide. "What the hell is that anyway?" Gabe wondered aloud.

The winter cold outside matched the emotional temperature of the room inside where Gabe and Alyssa had argued just an hour before. Something had happened at work that had reminded his wife of some past misdeed Gabe had committed. She had swept into the room ready for battle, needing to revisit the old grievance. Gabe believed that time should heal all wounds and had little patience for digging up hatchets that were better left buried. But Alyssa had an ax to grind, if one can be forgiven for such an egregious mixing of metaphors, and in minutes the couple had nearly been at each others' throats physically, and a thousand miles apart emotionally.

Gabe sighed. He wondered where Alyssa had gone. His imagination shook free from the leash of logic and bounded ahead into dangerous territory.

Where was she? *Who was she with*?

Gabe's mind created scenarios of betrayal and revenge being committed against him. A victim of his own morbid imagination, he clenched his fists in frustration and fought the lump setting up camp in his throat. As tears blurred his vision, he reached for the whiskey bottle hidden in the bottom drawer of his desk. He skipped the formality of a glass. As he tried to drown his fears, he noticed again the red thing in the snow.

He emptied the bottle and—like a child continually returning to a cupboard in search of nonexistent treats—Gabe felt around in his desk drawer again. His fingers found no miraculous second bottle but instead closed around the butt of his handgun. It was a Glock 22 purchased 'for protection.' Gabe idly hefted the weapon and listened to the goading whisper of snow against the window pane. Every time he glanced outside his eyes sought out the red thing.

A scarf; it has to be, he thought. The sound of tires crunching snow shifted Gabe's attention back to his own inner turmoil.

Alyssa burst into the house and brought the winter with her. She eyed him frostily as she unzipped her parka.

"Where have you been?" Gabe asked. He held the Glock out of view behind his hip. Alyssa curled her lip defiantly. Gabe trembled a little; she was more beautiful with her face twisted in a scowl than most women were when they smiled.

"I just want to know where you ran off to." Gabe fought to stay calm, "Seems like every little thing sets you off lately."

"I'm tired of your drinking Gabe," his wife announced, "Absolutely sick to death of it, in fact."

"Hey everybody has their vices."

"Well, I think that's just super, Gabe," Alyssa retorted with brittle politeness. "So what if I told you *my* vice is hooking up with Chuck from your work?"

Gabe remembered the pang of jealousy he'd felt as Alyssa giggled at all of Chuck's jokes at the office Christmas party. Now, an image of the pair entangled in bed sheets assailed his mind. He mentally crumpled up the image and tossed it aside but the next image that popped into his brain lacked the protective buffer of the bed sheet. Gabe groaned aloud and gritted his teeth.

"Hey, everybody has their vices," Alyssa mocked. She gave an exaggerated shrug and held out her hands as if to say, '*Nothing you can do about it, now is there*?'

Gabe raised the Glock and shot her in the face. Now all the x-rated scenes in his mind had turned into snuff porn. Suddenly nauseated, Gabe fled the house and stumbled into the back yard, his heart pounding.

Where's that red thing at? He suddenly felt an overwhelming desire to find the red thing in the snow. Everything else could wait; right now he needed to satisfy his curiosity. There was safety in this mundane endeavor. The winter wind howled in his face and blasted him with icy throwing-stars, no two alike, but he kept scanning the ground.

Much to his chagrin, the mysterious red object that had gotten into his head was nowhere to be found. Gabe squinted in the approaching dusk but saw nothing out of the ordinary. Sure that he now stood exactly where he'd seen the splash of color from his window, he paused and gazed back at the house. Inside, his wife lay in a growing puddle of red. Out here, Gabe was surrounded by arctic white. So where was the red thing in the snow?

Gabe glanced down at the gun and realized the truth of what he'd been looking at all afternoon. Could something echo back from the future? Could an object leave an afterimage before it even happened? Gabe raised the Glock and mashed the barrel into one nostril. He pulled the trigger and completed his own self-fulfilling prophecy.

The red thing in the snow came out of his head.

Icy Fingers

Melissa L. Webb

"Mommy, who is Jack Frost?" Abigail asked, as she bounced up to her mother.

Her mom glanced down at the six-year old. "What, Honey?"

Abigail stared up at her, hands on hips. "Mommy, I said, who is Jack Frost?"

Her mother let out a small chuckle. "Why, he's the one who brings the cold weather."

Abigail cocked her head slightly and frowned. "He does?"

Her mother nodded sagely. "Yes, he does. When Winter begins to show, you know Jack Frost has been working late at night."

Abigail thought for a moment. "What exactly does he do, Mommy?"

"Well, when he comes across a lake or a pond, he breathes on it with his icy breath."

Abigail's eyes lit up. "That's what makes the ice we skate on?"

Her mother nodded again. "Yes, and when Jack Frost steps across the ground with his chilly feet, snow appears in his path, turning it into a winter wonderland."

Abigail laughed in pure delight. "I love the snow, Mommy. It's my favorite thing in the whole world!"

"I know, Sweetie," her mother said and leaned down towards her. "But do you know what *my* favorite thing is? It's when I get up early in the morning and pull back the curtain. I love the ice that covers the window in beautiful patterns." Her mother smiled. "Jack Frost painted those pictures."

Abigail looked at the window behind her, at the morning ice that covered the pane. "He did that?"

"He sure did," her mother said, straightening up. "Jack knows how much people like it and how much they look forward to it every winter." She looked down at her daughter's smiling face. "Do you know what he is most famous for?"

Abigail's eyes widened. "No. What is it, Mommy?"

Her mother laughed and touched Abigail's nose lightly. "You know how some mornings you wake up and your nose is really, really cold?"

"Like it was this morning?"

"Yes, like this morning," Her mother told her. "When that happens, you know he's been visiting you."

Abigail was quiet for a moment. "So he's good, Mommy?"

Her mother looked down at her daughter. "Yes, Baby. He's very good," she reassured her. "He's a lot like Santa Claus."

Abigail nodded. "Okay, Mommy. If you say so," she told her mom as she turned and headed back towards her room. "I guess it's true then," Abigail spoke quietly to herself. "Jack Frost must be the man who comes in my room late at night with the icy fingers."

Fisher Creatures

Joe Dibuduo

"Something's moving on the mountain, let the dogs loose," I told Jacques. In response, he released our four hunting dogs. They charged up the snow-covered hill barking in joy to be in pursuit. They disappeared over the top of the hill and a few seconds later flashing lights lit up the sky; yelps of fear echoed over the hill.

"What'n the hell?" I said.

"I can't imagine; you know those dogs fear nothing."

"Yeah, but something's sure scaring the heck out of them now," I said. As we came to the top of the hill, we found the dogs rolling and barking on bloodstained snow.

"They must be in a feeding frenzy," I said.

"Probably caught a rabbit or two," Jacques said when he saw the pink snow.

I pointed to an area where the snow had melted into a three foot deep and a hundred foot long trench. "Do you think that ditch in the snow has anything to do with them yelping in fear?"

"Don't know, but looks like something melted that depression into the snow. Maybe it has something to do with those flashing lights we saw?" Jacques walked over to where the dogs ate, and in a shocked voice exclaimed, "Holy Cow, there were only four dogs when we started, and now there are eight."

"Must be somebody else's dogs got mixed with ours."

While we stood there scratching our chins trying to figure who had four dogs identical to ours, all eight suddenly coughed up a ball of flesh like material about six inches in diameter. The flesh sacs squirmed through the snow as though alive. We watched as each one blew up like a balloon and burst into an exact duplicate of the dog that choked it up. Eight dogs became sixteen.

Jacques and I looked at each other in amazement. "What'n the hell is going on?" I said.

"Don't know, but whatever the dogs got is gonna get us too if we don't get out of here."

I realized that Jacques was right; whatever infected the dogs could and probably would contaminate us too.

"We've got to get away," Jacques said, and started running down the hill.

He stopped halfway down and started coughing. A round ball of flesh leapt from his throat, squirmed around the snow for a few seconds, then expanded into an exact copy of Jacques. As soon as the duplication took place, both Jacques coughed up balls of flesh that went squirming through the snow. Terrified, I sped down the hill followed by thirty-two dogs and four Jacques.

Lucky for me, I didn't go near the area of melted snow that Jacques and the dogs did. I figured they must have gotten infected there. I had to warn the villagers before the infection spread, but I should have known I couldn't outrun the dogs. One bowled me over when it flew into my legs. Once I hit the ground, the dog stood over me dripping drool onto my face.

The dogs transmitted the infection at astonishing speed. One minute the dog drooled on my face, the next minute I was hacking up a ball of flesh that almost instantly became a likeness of me when it hit the snow—not only a likeness, but another me. My thoughts came in stereo and within a few minutes I doubled again and quadraphonic thoughts filled all my heads.

Dogs ran through the village infecting everyone. I doubled again and now used eight different brains to try and figure out if this was a gift or a curse. If it could be restricted somehow, it could be a boon for humanity.

Using all eight brains I concentrated extremely hard, trying to figure out how I could control the process. All eight of me coughed, and eight balls squiggled in the snow. Almost instantly I was thinking with sixteen brains. They came to the conclusion that if this contagion could be controlled, a single cow could be used to feed the world.

My thirty-two eyes turned skyward to see a large sausage-shaped craft hovering above the village. What at first looked like a cloud falling to the ground, turned out to be a silky substance that acted as a magnetic web attracting every living creature within fifty feet into it, including four of me and five of Jacques. Once full, the web was hauled back to the floating craft and its catch dumped onto a vast deck. The Jacques and four of me were gasping for air in the airless chamber, so were the animals taken along with us.

Two-legged creatures, including one of me and two of Jacques were picked up and thrown overboard. The disposed bodies spun in a circular motion until they hit the ground at speeds sure to kill. When Jacques and my duplicates hit the ground, all of us felt the pain and trauma of dying. But because there were so many of us, it was only like losing a finger or toe.

All other gasping life forms still on the ship were pushed into a hole in the floor, lined with ice, to keep them fresh. As my three remaining clones fought the creatures trying to throw them over the side, I heard one ask in perfect English, "Why do we need to throw the two-legged ones back?"

One of his mates with three rows of teeth answered in flawless French, "They're full of toxins, rather eat poison mushrooms than one of them any day."

Turnaround

Nathaniel Lee

This was the night of the Winter Festival. It was bitterly cold.

Emotions ran high, as they always did at this time of year. The days had grown shorter and shorter. The legend said the sun was being slowly devoured by an enormous cockerel, pecking away, bit by bit, at the light of the world. Most people laughed at that one, but it was hard to feel the same flippancy when you woke in the dark, worked in the cold, and went to sleep in the dark again. When it was hours after waking before the thin, reedy light of the winter sun slithered down, slipping through the trees like snow melting down your back; everyone was tense. The Festival was more necessary for the social release valve it provided than for its purported mystic properties.

They hung decorations. They brewed alcoholic beverages from what fruits and root vegetables they could spare. They hauled wood for the great bonfire and prepared the traditional twisted breads. They held the annual lottery. When the appointed night came, everyone was ready. More than ready; eager. Desperate!

The revelry lasted throughout the hours of darkness. The entire village danced and drank to excess, gathering in hooting crowds around the fire pit. Dance chains formed and broke apart, couples fleeing for a time into the dark, filled with need, only to return again to the fire and the food and the song. A little way apart, just where the shadows gained hold again, the pitted stone altar hunkered, cold and reptilian. No one looked at it, at least not for long. Stone should not be hungry.

Midnight, the fulcrum of the seasons, the changeover between ebb and flow, was the climax of the festival, the secret heart of this celebration and all celebrations. Everyone was quiet. Respectful. Hushed. Every sound seemed loud in the silence. When it was over, they washed the stone with buckets of warm water and stained the snow around it a flushed pink.

It was over, they knew. Now it was done, and the stars would turn their steps so the sun would rise again. They returned to their party with renewed fervor. No sleep tonight. They waited for the dawn, knowing the worst was past.

Morning came. The sun did not rise.

Final Exam

K.G. McAbee

Barry shrugged deeper into his threadbare hoodie as the icy winds whipped dead leaves from the trees. The ground was covered ankle-deep with thick crunchy layers of deadness. Snow was coming soon, though; that'd cover them.

Barry dug into the pocket of his jeans and pulled out the battered piece of paper, shined his little flashlight on it and studied the penciled map. The lines were faded, but he could tell he was almost there. He had to find this old place out in the woods; he had to. Even if the woman was a witch, even if his grandma would have tanned him good for even thinking of risking his mortal soul by going to her, he just had to.

He had to pass his final exam in algebra. He was already on academic probation. If he failed algebra this semester, he was out; no scholarship, no money, no college degree, no nothing. Then he'd be back home with his tail between his legs. No. No way he'd let that happen.

Whatever it took, he was going to pass algebra.

Even if it did risk his immortal soul, he thought with an uneasy laugh.

He sneaked another glance at the map, then looked up. There it was. A light shone through the trees, flickering in welcome. He'd found it.

The little cabin was old and looked ready to fall in. He stepped gingerly up on the cantilevered porch and gave a hesitant knock at the door.

It opened so quickly he started back and the desire to run, to forget this, to get away, almost choked him.

But he had to pass that final exam.

"Uh, Mrs. Mather?" he asked the tiny lady who peered out, her eyes milky with glaucoma.

"Yes, boy." Her voice was surprisingly deep. "What do you want from me?"

That stung, just a little. "What makes you think I want something?"

She cocked her head sideways and gave him a toothless grin. "No pretty boys come calling on me anymore; not for quite some years. That's why. Well, don't stand out in the cold."

Inside, the warmth hit him in the face like a shovel. Barry gasped and held his hands out to the fireplace.

"Well, boy? Ain't got all night. What is it?" She settled herself into an old rocking chair; a black cat jumped into her lap and began to purr, sounding like a distant freight train.

"Uh, well, you see," Barry began, shifting from one foot to the other. "I need—no, I've *got* to pass my algebra exam. And some of the guys in my dorm, they said you had a pill or something that'd help. Is that right?"

"Not a pill, no, not exactly." She rocked for a bit, absently stroking the cat. "You don't swallow it."

"Okay," he said. "What, then?"

"It goes in your ear."

"Ma'am?"

"Your ear, boy! You deaf as well as stupid?"

What had he gotten himself into? The guys, the stuff they told him; it had to be bull.

But if he didn't pass that exam...

"No, ma'am; I'm not deaf. How much?"

Her little milky eyes gleamed. "Come to your senses, hey? That'll be one hundred dollars cash, right here, right now. No arguments, no questions. You will know whatever you need to know for this examination, you will pass it with a guaranteed A." She held out one veined hand.

Barry pulled four twenties out of his pocket and laid them in her palm.

She looked down and shook her head. "You sure ain't good in math, are you, boy?"

Barry blushed and pulled out another twenty.

"Good enough." The money disappeared into her apron pocket. "Sit down on this here stool."

Barry sat on the three-legged wooden stool. He'd gone from freezing to hot and tried to edge it back from the fireplace.

"Right there!" she snapped. She reached up to a blue-and-white bowl on the mantelpiece and removed a small white object about the size of an elongated aspirin.

Before Barry quite knew what was happening, she'd stuck it deep inside his right ear. He shivered when he felt her ragged nail scratch against his skin.

She stepped in front of him. Sitting on the stool, he was eye-to-eye with her.

"What I just put in you will enter your brain," she said calmly.

Barry started to jump up but she slapped both hands, hard, on his shoulders.

"Listen, boy; these are things you need to know."

He settled back down, but his shivering grew worse. And what was happening to his ear? It must be bleeding where she scratched it; he could feel the blood flowing. It was itching, too; almost as if something was crawling on it.

"You feel it already, don't you?" she crooned. "It's inside you. I don't know what it is, mind you, a bug or a worm or something else from somewhere that ain't here. But it'll go inside your brain and it'll tickle them spots that needs ticklin', get 'em all sassy and full of smarts. You'll know stuff you never knew you knew."

Barry wasn't hearing her, not really. Instead, he was seeing things inside his head, algebraic manipulations, calculations, slope intercepts and point-slopes. Quadratic equations multiplied themselves in an instant and he saw answers in dazzling clarity.

"This is great!" Barry whispered.

"Yes, it is," said the old woman. "For now. When the worm gets hungry, though, it ain't near so nice. But don't worry; you won't last long after that. Not when the worm starts to feed..."

The Ice Weavers

Monique Bos

An earthquake juddered out from deep beneath the polar ice cap, rocketing up the Richter scale. Sudden canyons yawned in the permafrost. In Arctic mountains far from human eyes, the earth cracked and buckled.

A crevasse opened in the ice, stretching down to the belly of the planet, down to the quake's epicenter.

After the tectonic plates shuddered to a stop, a pair of slender, filigreed legs appeared at the crevasse's edge. Like blind worms feeling their way, they scrabbled greedily in the snow. Razor-wire hairs bristled. More legs slid onto the surface, followed by the curve of a large head. Multiple eyes surveyed the harsh contours of the peaks, the frigid brilliance of the stars, and the pristine imperiousness of snow.

The creature slipped out of the crevasse and into the night: a giant spider, as exquisite as a carving of ice or glass. She raised her front legs to test the direction of the wind as all around her spiderlings skittered up and over the rim of the earth.

***

The ice weavers rode in on the worst blizzard to hit Caribou Trails, Alaska, in more than a decade. They uncoiled their frost-limned spinnerets into the wind, tucked themselves under the cover of the cold front, and glided into town on legs as gracile as parachutes.

***

A nearly imperceptible lightening of the sky signaled day. Angel Stark opened her eyes expecting variations of gray: walls, snowdrift shadows, clouds, ceiling. Instead, she saw silver.

Her bedroom seemed to drip with icicles. She sat up, holding the blankets around her, and looked at the ribboned layers of ice that surrounded the bed and reflected light from the small lamp she kept lit in a corner. She thought drowsily that the window must have broken, but then she realized that although she was cold—she didn't think she'd been warm in the year and a half she'd lived in Caribou

Trails—she wasn't freezing. She couldn't see her breath. The glass was unmarked by fissures, and she could feel the generator thrumming beneath the buzz of the house's heating system.

Angel pulled her flannel pajama sleeve down over her fist and reached out toward the closest filament. It rebounded slightly from her touch with an elasticity she had never seen in ice.

She moved to withdraw her arm, but the flannel stuck. She tried to peel the fabric away, but every motion seemed to snare more fibers, and then her other sleeve brushed the strand of ice and held fast too.

Angel squatted on the bed and tugged. The ice seemed to give a little, to bow toward her, and then it sprang back. She leaned all her weight onto her heels, arching away from it, and both sleeves tore at the same time with such force that she toppled over.

At least she was free, she thought. She began to sit up but sharp, bright pain shot into the side of her head. Twisting around, she realized that strands of her hair had caught on another icy filament that coiled horizontally around her bed. She could see the scissors on the desk, where she'd left them the previous night after cutting out some letters for the school bulletin board. But strands of ice crisscrossed the space between the bed and the desk. She gritted her teeth and began to yank the trapped hairs out of her skin, a few at a time.

Between bursts of agony, she tried to comprehend this strange indoor ice storm that had encircled the bed. She might be able to break out if she had a hammer, she thought, or a saw; but her tools were in the next bedroom, even less accessible than the scissors.

Her arm, bare where the pajama sleeve had torn, bumped against the ice as she reached for her hair. Dry cold burned through her skin. She knew she'd been careful, and she thought dubiously that the frozen gossamer line must somehow have swayed toward her. She tried to look around but couldn't manage, and in the attempt her foot came perilously close to another strand.

She suddenly felt that she was in the center of a massive spider web. As soon as she thought so, she recognized that the ice surrounding her had the texture and strength of silk. Another strand stirred across from her, as if animated by an invisible breath, and Angel pulled her leg back just in time to avoid being caught.

This can't be a spider web, she thought, it makes no sense,

spiders don't grow this large, and they can't produce ice—

But she saw, edging out from the closet door, a pair of slender filigreed legs. In the darkness that should have held only her clothes and shoes and laundry hamper, light refracted off myriad eyes.

Angel screamed and began to thrash. Ice weavers slid out from behind the curtains, from the bathroom, from beneath her desk. They flowed toward the bed as her flailing limbs battered the silk and stuck to the strands, as she twisted and tossed and trussed herself up.

Within a few minutes, Angel Stark had stopped shrieking and fighting. An ice-wrapped mummy hung from the web that surrounded the bed. The weavers took turns feeding, and when they slipped out of the house, they left behind her shell, brittle and fragile as glass.

***

Throughout Caribou Trails, ice weavers emerged in the wake of the blizzard, gliding out of chimneys, pouring out of doors, sliding from windows. Plump and sated, they glittered in the night-dark Alaskan noon as the matriarch raised her front legs, testing the direction of the wind.

Alchemy

M.R. Shane

There was yelling. Lots of yelling.

Kylie expected it.

She covered her ears with her hands and braced for the smack across her ears.

"Where is he?"

She whimpered and held her fetal position on the bed until the stinging was too great. Then, she pointed towards the door.

"Darryl's out there? What the hell?" her Ma yelled.

She cracked an eye, rocking and watching as Ma ran for the door, then tumbled out in her tattered robe and slippers.

"Darryl!"

The morning wind howled and whistled like a hungry wolf. It came inside and bit her with its cold teeth.

Ma stood in the doorway, ignoring the snow curling around her like a ghostly mist and piling at her feet.

"When did he go out there?"

"I don't know," she lied.

Ma scowled then reached over to the bench and pulled on her coat and boots. She slammed the door behind her.

Her voice outside sounded muffled; the thick log cabin walls and the wind insulated Ma's screams.

Kylie began to cry. The tears were not for her brother. They were for her skin that would welt and bleed that night from the lashes. *I'm sorry, Ma.*

But, she wasn't. Not really.

She'd read it in a science book once. Nature could change things alchemically into something else. Dirt into flowers. Food into energy. Sky into rain.

She'd seen how raindrops from the dark thundering sky could land on the window and morph into ice crystals as beautiful and delicate as a ballerina's satin slippers.

Then, she thought about the ice.

Winter is like fire. It purifies. Kills the bad things. Then, they come back fresh and green, and pretty.

She had waited for the trees to shed their clothes and stand naked against the wind and snow—waited for the time when her bouquet of dead roses on the sill were frozen with dripping clots of ice.

It took lies to get him to go with her to the creek, sneaking out with only the quiet fat moon to see. She told him about Ma's locket that she'd borrowed and dropped while crossing. "She'll kill me. You have to—"

He'd said she'd owe him extra favors that night.

She nodded and urged him to hurry.

He was five feet out, a big heavy clod of flannel and meat, headed for the gold object, when the ice made a loud snap and swallowed him into the icy current below.

She stood there watching as he fumbled for a hold.

The gruff scream hurt her ears. "Help me, Kylie!"

But, she stood and stared, waiting for him to drop into the cauldron, so he could be cleansed and become a better thing.

It seemed to happen all at once. His blue eyes turned wide and glassy, and his red fingers lost their grip.

Then, he was gone.

"Amen," she whispered to the congregation of squirrels and deer that she knew were hiding just behind the stand of spruce in the distance.

***

Hours later, Ma came back sweaty and shivering. There were no lashes that night. There was silence. Ma eyed her like a bug, like something that she couldn't decide if she should squash or fry and eat with the leftover rice and beans.

That evening, when the embers of the fire were down to a slow orange crackle, there was a knock at the door.

Ma motioned for her to open it.

She shook her head.

No.

Before Ma could scold her for not moving, the door flew open.

It was him, but she didn't know it at first.

His skin was as white as the fresh snow, and his eyes were as dark as shiny pieces of coal. He was different now. Changed.

But, he wasn't a pretty new thing. He was a frozen dead

thing with ugly blue lips curled into a snarl.

Somehow, she knew that he wouldn't hurt her now—

—not in the way he had before.

This time, he would kill her.

Winter is like fire. It purifies. Kills the bad things.

And she had been bad. Very bad.

Stranded

Geoff Bagwell

I left work at lunchtime. An hour later, I was asleep in bed. When the telephone woke me, I peeled off the wet flannel, leaving ice-cold dampness on my forehead.

"Hello?"

"Jan, it's me."

Richard's company has large open-plan offices. Usually when he calls I can barely hear him.

"Is everything all right? It's quiet there."

"Er, yeah."

Er?

"Richard?"

"I called you at work. They said you had a migraine."

The first few hours of an attack are like the Fourth of July in my head. Once I've slept, though, the party's over, leaving just the dull ache of the morning after.

"It's okay now," I said. "Still looking forward to tonight."

"Ah."

"Ah?" Richard never forgets our anniversary.

"Open the bedroom curtains."

I briefly wondered how he knew they were closed, then I got up and opened them.

Snow. A blur of fist-sized flakes blowing in every direction, like pillows exploding in a wind tunnel.

"Jeeezus."

"Yeah - *Jeeezus*," Richard said. "And I'm stranded."

"What?"

"There was a weather warning and we were sent home."

I groaned. "But you're not here."

He explained although I'd already guessed. He stayed to finish what he was working on, public transport had shut down, and now he was stuck in the city while I was in the suburbs with a candlelit dinner for one.

"What are you going to do?"

"I don't have much choice."

My husband is a methodical man. In a crisis, he lists the options before selecting the least sensible.

"Trevor the security guard lives round the corner," he said. "I could sleep on his floor."

"Good idea."

"Or I could find a hotel."

"Even better," I said.

"Or I could try walking home."

I looked out the window. "Richard, don't try walking home."

"Okay," he said. "I'll call you later. Oh, happy anniversary."

***

I woke up cold and groggy - I'd fallen asleep again. But why were the curtains framed in harsh white light? I checked the clock.

Eight-thirty in the morning!

I'd slept through the night. Then I remembered taking the Migra-Soothe. They knock me out like Mike Tyson.

I pulled on my robe and opened the curtains. Snow, several feet deep, covered everything, and kids—and a few dads—were riding sleds, throwing snowballs at each other, and throwing snowballs at a snowman the frantic sledders were skidding to avoid.

I went downstairs to our kitchen phone and hit the messages button.

'*You have no new messages*.'

I called Richard's office. It rang for a long time before the call was automatically transferred.

"Acumen Assurance."

"Trevor? It's Jan Carver."

"Hi, Jan. Everything all right?"

I felt a twinge of panic at the concern in his voice.

"Did Richard stay with you last night?"

"No. I offered but he said he was fine."

"Okay, I'll try his mobile. Thanks."

I found my own mobile and checked the Inbox.

Nothing.

Why hadn't he called? Whatever Richard decided to do, he would have let me know.

If he could.

I pushed the thought away and rang his mobile. Eight rings later, it went to voicemail.

"Richard, it's me. Please call and tell me where you are."

The panic was growing. Somehow I ignored it and made more calls.

I tried the work friends I had numbers for. Each said the same thing: Richard was still working when they left and they had no idea where he was.

Next, I called the two hotels near his office. He wasn't at either of those.

Something terrible had happened. I could feel it. I picked up the phone again and made one final call. A woman answered.

"Woodbridge Police, can I help you?"

"I'd like to report my husband missing."

"When was he last seen?"

"Yesterday afternoon."

"Ah."

Déjà vu struck me. "Ah?"

"Under twenty-four hours and he's not missing."

"But he is."

"Not officially."

"But—" I trailed off, not knowing what to say.

"To report someone missing," she said, "you have to come here and fill out a form. If you do that now, I can alert our patrol officers as soon as it's twenty-four hours."

"I'm on my way."

Outside, the street was still full of people. Avoiding both snowballers and snowballs, I took out my mobile and tried Richard's number again.

I didn't notice it at first. My attention was on the hopeless ringing tone in my ear, praying Richard's voice would cut it short.

Then it struck me. A change. The screams and shouts of excited kids gradually fading.

I turned and saw one of the dads, Mike Saunders from next-door-but-two, on his knees. He had one hand raised in the air; the other gripped the side of his head.

He's hurt, was my first thought. Then his daughter, Ellie, did the same—dropped to her knees and put her hand to her head.

Suddenly, I realized. Mike's hand was raised for silence. The other was cupped around his ear. He and Ellie were listening.

And then I heard it too.

My arm filled with lead and fell to my side. My legs turned

to rubber—yet somehow they carried me into the road.

Towards Mike and Ellie.

Towards a faint, tinny ringtone, a now tragically ironic version of *The Sun Ain't Gonna Shine Any More*.

Towards the snowman.

Richard had tried to walk home after all.

The Blood God

E.J. Tett

"Hot cocoa," he said, handing her the mug with a smile.

"Thanks, Marky," Stella replied.

Marcus watched as she sipped the drink he had made. "Is it ok?" he asked. "Did I make it ok?"

"Mm, yeah it's great," she said. She gave him another smile and then fell silent.

"Really?" Marcus asked. "Or are you just saying that?"

"It's fine," Stella said, smiling briefly again.

He wondered if her smiles were real or if they were just to keep him sweet. She still had her woolly hat and gloves on and Marcus knew she'd leave at the first chance she got.

He wrung his hands nervously and then perched himself on the edge of the coffee table, glancing towards the window and at the ice forming on the inside of the pane. "My mom used to make cocoa," he said. "It really warms you up inside."

"It sure does," Stella said, again with the fake smile.

Marcus felt a flutter of excitement when she looked at him; her eyes were as grey as ice.

"I'm glad you like it," he said. "I put blood in it."

Stella had the mug halfway to her lips. "Blood?" she repeated.

Marcus nodded. "Not mine," he said quickly. "But uh… you can try it if you like?"

He tried to work out the expression on Stella's face. "You put blood in my drink?" she said slowly. "You're serious?"

"You said you liked it," Marcus said. "You said it tasted great!"

"You freak!" Stella cried, getting to her feet quickly. She dropped the mug to the carpet with a look of disgust on her face.

Marcus made a grab for her arm as she passed. "Don't go," he said.

"Get off me," Stella growled and she shook her arm free from his grasp.

"No," Marcus said, standing up and snatching at her arm again, pulling her back towards him. "I said don't go."

"Marcus, you're freaking me out," Stella said, trying to prise his hand from her arm. "I want to go home!"

"You're not the one, are you?" Marcus said, curling his lip in disgust. "How many more do I have to go through before I find her?!"

Stella pulled her glove off with her teeth and then dug her fingernails into Marcus's hand around her arm. He cried out in irritation and back-handed her across the face, watching as she fell to the floor with a thud. "How many more?!" he yelled again.

Marcus looked at Stella and then felt a shiver run down his spine. He knew it came from more than just the cold in the room. "No," he said. "I don't want to!" He looked back at the statue sitting on his mantelpiece. "I won't," he told it.

The statue stared at him with stone eyes set in a baboon face. They bored into him. Marcus winced and turned back to Stella, grabbing her by the hair as she tried to get up. She screamed so he shook her roughly. "Shut up," he said.

"You're hurting me," Stella sobbed. "I don't know who you think I am! Just let me go!"

Marcus dragged her over to the statue and pushed her face close to its. "I can't," he said. "He won't let me."

"It's a statue," Stella said, hitching in a breath. "Please!" Stella screamed as Marcus pulled her forcibly towards the back door and he tightened his grip on her hair in irritation. With a yell, he pulled the door open and threw Stella out into the snow. He slammed the door and leaned back against it.

The statue stared impassively ahead though Marcus still felt as though it looked at him. He closed his eyes briefly and when he opened them again he spotted Stella's woolly hat in the middle of his floor. He went to pick it up. The statue watched him.

"She won't go far," Marcus said. "She'll get lost, I'll get her back." He glanced up from the hat briefly and looked at the statue before clearing his throat. "She wasn't the right one anyway, she didn't want any blood!"

He knew the statue didn't care for his excuses. He had let Stella go when he could've used her. He should've done the same to her as the last girl, killed her and drained her dry… The statue needed blood.

"I'll get her back," Marcus said again. He walked over to the mantelpiece and reached out a hand tentatively to touch the statue. The stone was icy cold and Marcus could see cracks appearing. "You need blood," he said quietly, "Yes, I know. I'd give you mine if I could…"

Marcus sighed and moved his hand away. His house was getting colder and colder so he threw another log on the fire though it never seemed to do much good. He needed to find the statue its consort so that it'd leave him alone; he needed a woman as bloodthirsty as the God he served.

Marcus shivered and crouched by the fire to warm his hands. "I don't want it to be winter forever," he said, glancing up at the statue briefly. "I'll get her back. I promise."

Winter beneath the Tarp

Stephanie L. Morrell

Snow covered the plastic tarp protecting Jackie's backyard garden. She brushed it off with a gloved hand and noticed something moving underneath.

"What do I have living in my garden?" She spoke the words out loud to no one.

"Did you say something?" Garret approached his wife.

"Just talking to myself." She chuckled.

"That's nice." He gave his wife a soft kiss on the lips. "Do you need help with anything out here?"

"I'm fine." She saw a jerking motion beneath the blue canvas. "Did you see that, Garret?"

"See what?" He furrowed his brow.

"I've got some kind of animal living inside my garden." She bent down and poked her finger against the hard plastic covering, but there was no reaction. "I swear there is something under here." She looked up at Garret.

"Do you want me to take a look?" He got down on the ground beside her.

"That's alright. Winter will be over in a few weeks and I will be preparing the ground for spring." She stood up and brushed away the cold wet snow melting into the knees of her jeans. "I might as well wait till then."

"Are you sure?" He stood up with her.

"Positive." She nodded. "Did you still want to go out for dinner tonight?"

"Sounds good."

"Great. I'll be a little bit longer back here so you can shower first."

***

Jackie checked on the garden throughout the weeks and continued to hear something scurrying around. One night, when Garret was working late, she went out back to take a closer look.

"You're probably cold, but God knows what you're doing

under there." She cut through the rope tying a corner down and then slowly lifted the tarp. "Anyone home," she asked while shinning a flashlight into the darkened garden.

There was no reply. The ground underneath the tarp was silent and still. Whatever was living in there had fallen asleep or relocated elsewhere.

"Come on little guy. Wake up and let me see you."

Jackie grabbed a stick from the ground and slid it into the garden. She moved it back and forth under the plastic covering and gasped as something latched onto it.

"Oh my God." The strength of the creature took Jackie by surprise.

She removed her hand from the stick and tried to pull it out from the darkness when teeth clamped onto her flesh. She screamed out in pain as her arm became saturated with blood.

Jackie used all of her might to break free, and with one last pull she did, but the creature was still attached. The back of its head was upright and Jackie could see that there was hair on its skull instead of fur. With one last effort she removed her arm from its grasp and realized that her hand had been devoured. All that was left was a bloody stump at the end of her wrist. She kneeled down on the cold winter ground and squeezed the boney area where her hand had once been.

"Somebody help me," she screamed out in terror and shock. "Help me."

Jackie started to inch away from the garden when a pale gangly limb reached out from under the tarp. It latched onto her open amputation and then quickly reeled her in. She began to kick and scream, but the creature's strength pulled her under and into the darkness. She opened her eyes wide and tried to take in the surroundings. The only things that she could make out were the eyes of the creature. They were bright red and feverish with hunger. Jackie opened her lips to call out but the creature cut her off. It pressed its mouth against her face and began to suck the flesh from her skull. It did this greedily until the only thing that remained of Jackie was a pile of disconnected bones.

***

Garret returned home from work and was surprised to discover that Jackie was not inside. He made his way to the back garden and frowned at her absence.

“What’s this?” He got down on one knee and examined the dark pool of blood seeping into the cold hard ground. “Jackie?” He surveyed the area with his eyes. “What the hell hap—”

Garret’s words were cut off as a pale white limb reached out from under the tarp and quickly pulled him under.

Snowmen

Doree Weller

"The snowman moved," Gladys said, face pressed to the frosty glass.

Herb didn't look up from his newspaper. "The snowman didn't move."

"It moved, Herb."

"Mmm-hmm."

Gladys turned away from the window and flicked the drapes closed so that it couldn't look in on her. She picked up a novel but couldn't get interested. She threw the book down and Herb looked up.

"What time are the boys due in?"

Gladys glanced at the clock. "About an hour. I'm going to make cookies."

Herb grunted as Gladys left the room.

When the bell rang a little over an hour later, Herb greeted Janice, Jack, and Ben. Gladys wiped her hands on a red dishcloth as she bustled out of the kitchen. She kissed Janice on the cheek before bending down to the boys' eye level. "I have cookies."

Ben and Jack raced to the kitchen, shoving one another the whole way.

"Thanks for doing this. Bill and I need a night out."

"You know we never mind watching the boys," Gladys said.

Janice hugged them both before driving away.

Herb and Gladys went into the kitchen, where Jack had managed to pour them both glasses of milk. He got most of the milk into the glasses, leaving only a few spatters on the kitchen table.

"Grandpa, can we have pizza for dinner?" Ben asked, grinning.

Soup bubbled in a pot on the stove. Herb looked at Gladys, and she shrugged. "It'll keep until tomorrow."

"Alright." Herb grabbed his jacket and keys. "Pepperoni and anchovies okay with everyone?"

"Ew, Grandpa. We don't like fishies on pizza." Ben made a

sour face.

"Okay, but if I can't have anchovies, I want lima beans."

"Grandpa," Jack said, drawing the word out.

Herb kissed Gladys and then the boys. "Be good."

The boys finished their cookies and wiped their mouths with their sleeves. "What do you want to do now?" Gladys asked.

"I wanna play in the snow." Ben bounced up and down in his chair.

"Yeah!" Jack agreed.

Gladys shot a nervous glance out the kitchen window. Her backyard should be safe. It was fenced, and there were no snowmen back there. Still, she hesitated before agreeing. She helped them on with their bulky winter clothes and sent them outside.

Gladys cleaned up the kitchen, keeping an eye out for the boys as they romped and rolled around in the back yard. The light faded as snow continued to fall.

The door flew open and a small snowman rushed inside. Gladys screamed and heard a buzzing in her ears. She shoved it, and it fell backward. The buzzing in her ears grew louder as the snowman got up and moved toward her again. Heart pounding, she grabbed the soup from the stove and flung it over the snowman. Snow dripped from it, but she grabbed her knife and started hacking the snow apart until the buzzing in her ears stopped. She looked up, and another snowman hovered in the doorway. She screamed and ran out of the room before realizing that the boys were in the back yard.

Clutching the knife in her shaking hands, she went back into the kitchen and peered through the window. Both boys were gone and the back gate was ajar. Heedless of snowmen, she rushed outside, screaming, "Jack! Ben!"

Snow filled her slippers, and melted snow puddled on the floor. She skidded across the linoleum and dialed 911. The police arrived in minutes, and she rushed to the door and outside before the police even stopped the car.

An officer got out of the car slowly but stayed by the door. "Ma'am, drop the knife."

"Hurry, you have to hurry. I don't know where the boys are. I don't know if the snowmen got them."

"Ma'am, drop the knife."

She threw the knife down. "Now will you help me?"

He approached slowly. “Ma’am, whose blood is that?”

“Blood? What blood?” She looked down at her blouse and scowled. “I don’t know. Maybe I cut myself. What does it matter?”

“Can I check the house?” he asked, drawing his gun out.

“Of course.”

The two officers went into the house and came out less than 5 minutes later, guns still raised. As they handcuffed her, one officer asked her, “Why did you kill the boy? Where’s the other one?”

“What are you talking about? The snowman attacked me.”

They found Ben a week later in a snowdrift down the street where he hid after watching Grandma kill Jack.

Winter Blues

Sean O'Connor

The problem is, I can never get to sleep in the winter. And it isn't because I'm too cold. No, that's never it. It's because people's attitudes are different in winter, and it really takes a toll on me during the day.

For instance, yesterday on the way to work, I bought the newspaper off the cashier. Instead of saying thanks once I'd given him the money, he simply muttered, "All you people are so tight, all you buy is the newspaper."

And then, at the office, Mary Jenkins from HR yelled at me because I was using the photocopier when she wanted it:

"James, you're always on that thing right when I want it!"

I mean, you can see what I'm talking about, can't you? Winter makes people crazy.

So that's why I've decided to kill the first person who annoys me today. I've put a knife in my suit jacket pocket, and the first person to say one mean thing to me, is getting it right between their eyes.

I went to the same corner store as yesterday. The winter chill went right inside my jacket and I trembled. The streets were covered in sleet, and every now and then someone just slipped right over. It was quite humorous, actually.

"One newspaper, thanks," I said to the cashier. It was the same guy from yesterday. He looked at me, holding out his palm. He didn't smile. With my spare hand I got the knife ready in my pocket.

When I placed the money into his hand he smiled. I loosened the grip on the knife.

"Thank you, sir," he said, putting the cash in the draw. "See you tomorrow."

So there'd been a slight change in attitudes from the cashier over night. Very well then, I'm sure I could find someone else with the winter blues.

I was waiting at the bus stop when a person pushed in front of me. Here we go! I felt excited at the prospect of a conflict.

"Excuse me," I said to the lady rugged up in a thick trench coat. "I think I was actually next in line."

I waited for her sarcastic or arrogant replay. I would put the cold knife in my pocket right through her left eyeball. It would be something!

But she grinned apologetically.

"Oh, I'm sorry, love. Here, go before me."

What was wrong with people today? It was winter, right?

As I entered work from the freezing outside, I greeted the receptionist. She had always ignored me previously, always too busy to reply to my greetings.

"Hi, how are you this morning?"

If she didn't reply: right between the eyes.

She glanced up. Her face was rosy from the chilliness. "Oh, hi, Mr. Anderson. Looking good today," she said, smiling as she went back to work.

Why won't anybody annoy me today! I clenched the knife in my pocket in frustration. The one day I actually have a counterattack for all the bad things that happen to me, and no one will take the bait?

I had one more chance. Mary Jenkins from HR. The one who'd blasted me yesterday for using the photocopier when she wanted to. I'd sit near her office, then, when I saw her heading to the photocopier, I'd dash over and use it first. That would be fun!

I waited for the first hour of the day. It was snowing outside the window again. Brilliant. It meant she'd be in even more of a bad mood.

Finally there was a squeak as her office door opened. Mary walked out, looking down at a bunch of papers she held.

Showtime! I hopped up from the coffee table I'd been sitting at and dashed to the photocopier. I just beat her to it. I lifted the lid, then started copying the first of fifty separate sheets.

"Excuse me," she said, glancing at the copier. I clenched my knife. A buzz went through me.

Then she saw who I was.

"Oh, hi, James. I wanted to apologize for attacking you yesterday. That was really uncalled for, and I should know that, being in HR." She stuck out her hand for me to shake and gave me a warm smile. "I'm sorry."

I looked at her hand. Frustration rumbled inside of me. My

hand was shaking on the knife. I pulled my hand from my pocket and …

Shook hers.

"No worries," I said, the knife still in the pocket. She grinned and took her papers back to her office.

No good, I thought, shaking my head on the walk home from work, my feet skidding on the icy streets. I shivered from the cold. This weather was doing me in. No good, no good, no good. Everyone's in such a … pleasant mood today. I had my head down in turmoil.

I bumped into someone.

"Hey, watch where you're going, idiot!" the man muttered to me, fog coming out of his mouth. "Damn idiot!"

He gave me a scowl and walked off.

I grinned in the winter mist. I caressed the knife in my pocket.

Score.

SPRING

Good Bait

Douglas J Lane

The Red Drum were running strong, and the one Tully hooked was a leviathan. Pull, crank, let it run, pull, crank—he danced the way his father taught him, wrestled the fish out of the water and up as it thrashed its body. As he maneuvered a net around it and heaved it over the rail, he eyeballed the thing. Fifty pounds? Not a record, but damned fine for April.

"Good bait," Harteford said beside him, admiring the fish. It was the third Tully had pulled that morning. "What are you using?"

Tully could feel the simmering envy in Harteford, whose hooks might as well have been snorkeling. "Do-it-yourself," he said. "Mullet, mackerel, a little shrimp, bloodworm, other bits." It was only half-true; no honor among fishermen where tricks of the trade were concerned. "If it keeps working like this, I might have a chance in competition this year. Take a prize or two. Maybe pull a record."

They stood at the end of the pier, the waves a watery heartbeat against the pilings. Despite the warmth and the cloudless sky, they were alone. Tully liked slow days. Too many amateurs clogged the pier once it got hot, tourists with no sense for angling. The bait shop kept a nurse on call for dealing with unwanted hand piercings.

"D'ja hear McKlusky's missing?" Tully asked.

Harteford's played out a little more line. "Damn. Really?"

"Yeah. Marion says he went up to Virginia to do some ice fishing in December. Didn't say where. Didn't come back. Cops are still looking."

"Damn," Harteford said again. "McKlusky sure knows how to catch a fish."

The Red Drum in the cooler, Tully dipped a hand into his bucket and fished out another chunk of bait. "He sure does." The barbed ends of his hooks slid silently into the flesh, which oozed from the perforations. He cast the line. Sinker and bait plunked into the waves twenty yards off.

"I hope nothing bad happened to him," Harteford said. "Though it might be easier for a guy to win a contest without him around."

Tully shot him a sideways glance. "The man could be at the bottom of a lake somewhere, and you're worried about a bass tournament?"

"I didn't mean anything by it," Harteford said.

"That's pretty callous. Marion is worried sick."

"Jeez, I'm sorry." Harteford sounded more like he was sorry he'd aired the thought, not the content. "It's just that he's been winning the thing for twenty years."

Harteford wasn't seasonal, but he'd only been a resident for a few years. He hadn't spent the previous two decades like the rest of them had, battling McKlusky, his secret fishing spot, year after year of prize bass. Tully and the other old-timers had reason for frustration. Coming from Harteford, it seemed unduly competitive.

They fished in silence a while longer before Harteford packed up. "Hope McKlusky turns up," he said by way of goodbye, annoyance in his voice. Tully listened to Harteford's footfalls as the man receded down the long pier. Then Tully's reel began to turn. Pull, crank, let it run, pull, crank. Whatever it was, it felt big. Record big. Tully could feel it fighting him in the undercurrent. The line pulled taut. He gave it slack, muscled the pole, could feel whatever was down there was turning, giving up.

The line snapped.

Tully sighed and reeled in the slack. He tied a new hook and sinker onto the ragged end of the wet line. He plucked a fresh piece of bait from the bucket and skewered it on the hook. The glint of sunlight off something in the bucket caught his eye. He wondered how he'd missed it.

The Drum might like something shiny, he thought.

He tied McKlusky's wedding band to the line and cast the freshly baited hook into the rolling sea.

April Showers

Scott Cole

April showers bring May flowers. That, my dear, is what they say. But I would like to see for myself, now that Spring is here.

Lie down now, won't you? I'll give you a hand. Careful now—don't let your hair get tangled in the ropes.

I've got a big bucket full of rain here. Needles and pins and pieces of glass. See how it sparkles, reflecting the light? Let's pour a little bit and see what happens.

It's beautiful, isn't it? See it glisten? See it shine?

Would you like some more? Yes, yes, of course you would. It must feel nice. Refreshing. Am I right? Careful there—be sure to close your eyes.

No, don't try to speak. Let's just listen to the sound of it. Hear the rain cascading down? Such a pretty sound.

Well, well. That was rather quick, wasn't it? Looks like the storm is over now. Did you enjoy it? I certainly did.

And look! What's that? Oh yes, a tiny flower! And there's another—a lovely little rose.

Would you look at that? Another little flower. And another! Everything's coming up roses! That's the saying, isn't it?

Oh, how beautiful, May. Don't you think? A bed of roses.

You, my dear, are a beautiful bed of roses.

In Bloom

Robert Essig

Oh, how Grace loved spring. What a wonderful season, the best time of year in her mind: the perfect weather, the last melting of the wretched snow-pack, and most of all, the flowers—fragrant, colorful and brilliant.

Grace was a bit of a green thumb, always had been. She planted bulbs after Halloween and sowed her special seeds just after the last spring frost.

Flowers were one thing, and then there were the vegetables and fruits to consider. Living just outside of Napa gave her a prime location to grow just about anything she wanted, and, with her special seeds, she grew a feast most people would gape at in awe, fruits and vegetables that rivaled the imagination and begged for just a taste.

It was important to save the seeds after eating the harvest, that way she had them for next year, because Grace was quite sure she would never cross paths again with the ancient man who gave them to her. He was a modern day wizard, to the best of her knowledge, who gave her a bounty of strange seeds and a series of instructions on just how to plant and fertilize them for an exotic yield.

She mulled over the seeds for a whole year before discovering that her husband and son had been driving into San Francisco to sow seeds of their own. What were supposed to be fishing trips turned out to be father/son homosexual escapades in underground bathhouses, fueled with booze and crystal meth.

After the police raided one of the drug addled sex parties, they were both arrested and spent the night in jail; Grace reluctantly bailed them both out the following day.

But that was another spring over ten years ago, the last spring of her former life, of the family she once thought she would grow old with and cherish forever.

The sun felt wondrous on her skin as she made the walk from her house to the greenhouse. There would be a wealth of beautiful flowers freshly bloomed for the arrangement she planned to showcase as the centerpiece for the dinner she was hosting with her romance-book-of-the-month club, as well as the flowers that would inevitably turn into exotic unimaginable fruits and vegetables.

Grace opened the door to the greenhouse inhaling the heady perfume of her babies. She liked to refer to her plants as such. It took quite a deal of care for the special seeds to grow, perhaps more so than that of a real baby.

"Hello, my pretties. How are we today?"

Sounds issued, like vines rubbing together, as the plants turned just slightly as if to face Grace as she entered. In some of them she could see the face through full leafy branches, but most had grown bountiful hiding the bodies that dwelt beneath.

Grace walked through her greenhouse, eyes buried deep within thickets of flora catching hers as she passed by, people suspended in an unnatural state, feeding her plants.

At the center of her lush indoor garden were her two favorite plants. Sprouting and wrapped tightly around her husband's and son's bodies were vines of a peculiar variety laced with lengthy barbs that stuck into their mummified skin. From the vines protruded stems that ended in the most magnificent blooms Grace had ever seen. They were so deeply red, they could be mistaken as black from a distance, and they were always the talk of her famous centerpieces.

With a gesture, she open and closed her shears making a metallic sound, and the plants knew what that meant. A tear rolled down her husband's face, hardly visible beneath the gnarled vines. She found the most beautiful of his flowers and dug her nose in, deeply inhaling a sweet perfume only her special flowers were capable of, eyes closed as she relished in her organic love affair.

At the base of the stem, she clipped the flower. He quivered and a whimper escaped from a mouth that had long since grown a thicket of vine.

Grace placed the flower in her vase, a drop of blood from the cut stem landing solitarily on the floor. She would have to bleed one of her babies so her flowers would have liquid nourishment to keep them lively for her dinner party.

Aftermath

Geoff Bagwell

Smith eased the door closed behind him, careful not to wake Elizabeth and the baby. After another bad night, they were finally asleep and the longer they stayed that way the better. These days, sleep was the only refuge from the nightmare.

Outside on the pavement, he stopped. The street was deserted. Over his shoulder hung the rifle he'd found last year, next to the body of a dead soldier. The empty street, together with the rifle, made him feel . . . well, maybe not safe, but safer.

Feeling safe was a luxury of another age, like the assumption that the flashpoints of the world's bloodiest conflict would only ever be seen on a television screen. Those things were gone forever, since the brief respite between the Cold War's end and the Holy War's beginning had turned out to be just that—a respite.

But the winter had been long and many had died. Of the survivors, most were sick and weak.

And in the land of the frail, Smith thought, *even a thirty year old accountant can survive.*

And he had to. They had a baby.

He scanned the row of Victorian terraced houses. He thought he saw a movement in a window and frowned. He stared, concentrating on the laced net curtains, assessing the risk. His finger crept towards the trigger of the rifle and rested there.

Nothing. Just his imagination. Slowly, he took his finger from the trigger guard and allowed the tension to ease from his shoulders. He began to walk.

A casual glance and the street appeared as it had when they moved in—typical London terraced housing, a mile south of the Thames, built for the poor of the nineteenth century, inhabited by the wealthy of the twenty-first.

Except it wasn't the same. According to Smith's watch—analogue, of course, now that semiconductor and quartz based devices no longer worked—it was ten past eleven in the morning. Despite the time, a dusty grey haze hung in the air; this twilight now passed as daylight. And in another two hours, darkness would begin closing in, until a starless night smothered everything by two o'clock in the afternoon.

Smith walked on. Past front gardens where shriveled flowers had fought to root, then failed to bloom; past trees, either diseased, dead, or dying; and past animals, skulking in shadows. Most of these were pets—or their mutant offspring—cats and dogs who were nowadays more likely to be food than fed. Left to fight for survival amongst the rats and other vermin, they stood little chance, their hunting genes lost long ago to domestication.

Smith reached the Costcutter. After a quick glance over his shoulder, he went inside.

Sanjeev had been sitting on a stool behind the counter. Now he stood, his right hand instinctively resting on the AK-47 hanging across his body.

"Brian, my friend. How's it going?" Apart from Elizabeth, Sanjeev was the only person who spoke to him like this. Civility and manners were a waste of energy, better conserved for the effort of staying alive. "How are Elizabeth and the baby?"

"They're fine.

Sanjeev kept smiling, but his eyes held only pity. These were not the days to start a family. "So what do you need?"

Smith glanced around. The store was small, little more than a newsstand now, but it had once sold all the essential groceries. Now its shelves were hopelessly barren. He turned back to Sanjeev. "What have you got?"

The smile faded and died. "Wait."

Sanjeev went through a door behind the counter. When he returned, he held a cardboard box. He placed it on the counter and picked items from it, one at a time. "Nappies—one pack; wipes—two packs; baby food—four jars."

"That's it?" Smith said.

Sanjeev shrugged apologetically. "That's it."

Smith thrust his hand into his jacket and pulled out a fistful of currency: Elizabeth's wedding ring, a gold chain which had belonged to her mother, a pair of gold earrings, and other stuff he hadn't even wanted to look at. "Is it enough?" he asked.

Sanjeev nodded. "I'm sorry," he said as he took them.

"Yeah," Smith said. "We all are."

The house was quiet when he got back; Elizabeth and the

baby were still asleep. He trod softly along the hall, then slowly climbed the stairs. In the bedroom, he stood beside the bed.

Thin grey light crept in around the curtains. Mother and baby lay face to face, and even in sleep Smith saw the anxious lines creasing Elizabeth's forehead. Then he shifted his gaze to the daughter he himself had delivered three months ago.

Lying on her side, her profile was one of delicate perfection: the graceful upturned nose; the tiny ear like exquisitely carved mother-of-pearl; the kiss of lips; the gentle swell of her cheek. Something hard knotted in Smith's throat and, though agnostic in belief, he suddenly understood how many could only attribute such beauty to a benign creator.

Then she moved. Slowly she settled onto her back.

And now Smith saw the other head. It sprouted from the crook of her neck, puffy and bulbous like a tumor, with empty eye sockets and twisted features. Its skin was translucent, like an over-inflated balloon, and just below the surface a network of veins throbbed and pulsed, mocking Smith's hope that it would shrivel up and die.

He turned away. He swallowed before the lump in his throat could become the sob he felt rising up from his guts.

Don't wake them. Sleep is the only escape.

And then the other thought came, as it so often did.

The nuclear winter was bad; but it will be nothing compared to the nuclear spring.

Wet Clothes

Adrian Ludens

"I need your help Joel! It's too heavy for me!"

I groaned and staggered against the side of the car while my son giggled. "I'm still too little to carry that, Daddy!" he admonished me. I straightened and lifted the basket of laundry and pointed my chin toward the door. "Can you open that for me?"

My son bounded toward the entrance with the kind of energy only five-year-olds seem to possess. He grunted with effort but succeeded in pulling the door open without help. Joel pressed his back against the door to hold it open and eyed me critically as I hefted the overflowing basket past him.

"You have a big belly Daddy," my son announced candidly.

"You have big ears," I teased. "But I love you anyway."

I surveyed the interior of the laundromat. A Somali woman folded clothes near the dryers. Behind the counter perched an ancient woman who looked like she'd seen it all. I plopped the basket onto the floor in front of a row of dingy top-load washers. I separated the whites into one load and crammed the colors and darks together in another. With Joel bounding ahead of me, I plodded toward the old woman behind the counter. She pointed toward an automatic change machine on the wall before I could reach her.

"You know what this is?" I asked Joel in an excited whisper. My son shook his head. "It's a machine that lets you win money. You have to feed in a dollar first and then you find out what you win." I held a dollar out to Joel and he snatched it. He fed the bill into the slot. When the four quarters rattled into the dispenser Joel's eyes lit up and he eagerly scraped up the coins with his fingers.

"I got four moneys!"

"I can't believe it! You put in one and got four back?" I feigned disbelief. Joel nodded emphatically. "Try it, Daddy! Maybe you can win like me." I fed my three remaining dollars into the change machine and we exclaimed over our 'winnings.'

I dumped a scoop of blue and white powder into each washer and fed the machines half of our quarters. I noticed the Somali woman leaving as I gave Joel a quarter for the gumball machine.

Time passed. I lounged against the washer and idly watched the cars passing on the street outside. I glanced at the time. The loads would be finished washing in a couple minutes. Once I had moved our wet clothes into the dryers, I thought we'd make a quick trip to the mall so Joel could see the Easter Bunny. But after what happened next, we abandoned those plans.

"Do I really have big ears Daddy?" Joel suddenly wanted to know.

"Huge; like Dumbo. If you learned how to flap them, you could probably fly."

My son eyed me critically. "Who's Dumbo?"

"An elephant."

Joel's mouth dropped. "I don't have elephant ears!"

I laughed. "Okay, maybe they're not that big. But they are as big as a rabbit's."

"A rabbit's?" The boy sounded incredulous. He also sounded as if he loved every moment of our silly conversation.

"You bet. Like the..." I paused and stared out the laundromats' front window in amazement. "Like the Easter Bunny's." I finished the sentence just as a guy dressed up in a pink and white Easter Bunny costume limped in through the front door. He carried an old-fashioned wicker picnic basket with a lid and approached the row of washers. I grinned at the guy but he didn't notice. One cloth ear stood straight up but the other flopped down sideways. He wore a purple vest and bow tie over the fake white fur. An eternal grin spread across the costume's face.

"Daddy, look!" Joel's mouth hung open.

"You can go say 'hi' to him but make sure you mind your manners." Joel scampered down the aisle. The washers buzzed about three seconds apart and I was momentarily distracted by the task of removing the wet clothes into my laundry basket. When Joel returned, he looked dazed and all color had drained from his face. "I want to go home Daddy. Right now."

"Didn't you get to meet the Easter Bunny?" I asked.

"Yes. I want to go home now." I was about to explain that we needed to dry our clothes first but Joel turned and marched straight out the front door. I hoisted the heavy basket of wet clothes and tromped after him. As I passed the guy in the bunny suit, I considered asking him what had happened. He stood before his washer seemingly oblivious to my presence so I moved on. I looked around for help but the place was empty. Even the immovable old Sphinx behind the counter had disappeared. I decided to talk to Joel in the car and, if the guy had been a creep, I'd come back in and have a chat with him.

Outside, I unlocked the car and helped my son onto his booster seat. I buckled him in and gently asked, "What happened buddy?"

His face still ashen, Joel held out his hand. His palm was sticky with what looked like blood-smeared jelly beans. "Did the Easter Bunny give you those?"

"Yes." he whispered. Tears trickled down my son's cheeks and he trembled. "I don't like the Easter Bunny. I saw him reach into his basket and pull out a long messy, drippy thing with an empty face on it. He put it in the washing machine."

I didn't understand and blundered into the next question. "What do you mean, 'an empty face on it'?"

Joel stared into my eyes. In his gaze, I saw the utter loss of innocence. "Daddy, the Easter Bunny was washing his person skin."

Fertilizer

Monique Bos

Father Lester Warren was a pedophile.

And to think she'd never guessed. Mary Grace scrubbed irately at the kitchen counter. She still wouldn't know if she hadn't popped back into his study to ask if he needed anything before she left to visit her sister Flo in Coral Gables. She always went for a week this time of year, before the kids came on Spring Break and trashed the beaches. The father had said he was meeting with the altar boys, so she'd thought nothing of bursting through the closed door. But Mikey Doyle was the only one in the room, and he'd looked at Mary Grace with such an expression of mingled shame and relief that, although she hadn't caught the priest with his trousers down, so to speak, she realized she'd interrupted just in time.

"Do you want a ride home?" she asked Mikey.

"Thanks, yeah, Mrs. O'Murphy, that would be great," the boy said. Father Warren refused to meet Mary Grace's gaze.

She hadn't tried to pump the boy for information. He ought to talk to a trained psychologist, she told herself, not some busybody housekeeper who should have realized long ago what was going on. All she said, as she turned into the lane where the Doyles lived, was, "Young Michael, if anything happened with the Father that shouldn't, anything you might feel ashamed about, you understand me, I just want you to remember it wasn't your fault."

His face turned such a bright red, that for a nerve-wracking moment, she thought he might cry. Instead he bit his lip and nodded, thanking her in a faint voice—for the ride or the advice, he didn't specify—before he jumped out of the car.

Mary Grace went home to scrub her immaculate cottage and ponder. She had no evidence to present to legal or ecclesiastical authorities, no proof. Just the faces of the man and the boy, and air so thick, even Jackie Chan couldn't have karate-chopped through it.

Finally, she called Father Warren. Said she needed to make confession a final time before she left on vacation and would he mind terribly running up to her cottage because she was in the midst of packing.

He said that would be fine, and, in fact, he'd been about to call because he wanted to discuss something with her. "Synchronicity," he said with a nervous laugh.

Seated at her kitchen table, he declined her offer of coffee or tea but accepted a cookie. "Before I hear your confession," he started, twisting his napkin, "I just wanted to say—er—today, when you saw me with Mike Doyle, you may have gotten the wrong idea."

"What idea would that be?" She crossed her arms and leaned against the stove.

"It may have seemed...it's possible...Well, it may have looked as if we were about to...you know...but there was nothing wrong. Nothing that I—but I'd told you a fib, that I was meeting with all the altar boys. Really it was just Mike. He'd asked to talk to me alone, you see, and I wanted to respect his privacy."

He looked up at her with a face so bovine and pathetic that if he had been anything else, anything but a predator of children, she might have pitied him.

"You were going to hurt that boy if I hadn't interrupted," Mary Grace said.

His fingers rattled against the tabletop. "Hurt him? Hardly. He enjoyed—"

"No," she said, "I'm quite sure he didn't. And now that I know what you are, I can't let you hurt more children."

She stepped behind him and plunged a syringe filled with cleaning fluid into his neck.

***

"Your number showed up in our search of the phone records," said the detective, who'd identified himself as DiGrassio. "You apparently were the last caller to talk to Father Warren before he disappeared."

Mary Grace nodded and topped off his coffee. "I wanted to remind him about a few things before I left for Florida. When to water the plants, what day the milk comes sort of thing. He's not good with details."

"How long have you known the father?"

"Three years this August," Mary Grace said promptly.

"He hired you to keep house?"

"Oh, no," she said, scooting the plate of cookies toward the detective. "I've been the parish housekeeper for more than fifteen years. I guess you could say he inherited me."

"Were you aware," DiGrassio asked, "that several families had recently filed complaints against him? There were allegations of improper conduct. With, well, with certain of the altar boys."

"I wasn't aware of complaints."

He took a cookie and studied her, reading into what she hadn't said. "Did you ever notice anything suspicious?"

"I never caught him doing anything specific. All I knew was what my gut told me," she said. "I just tried to make sure not to leave children alone with him behind closed doors, is all."

The detective nodded and looked out the window. "That's a gorgeous butterfly garden you have back there," he said.

Mary Grace beamed. "Yes, it's really blossomed this year, hasn't it? I put it in just before I went to Florida, and I couldn't believe how large and healthy the plants had grown already by the time I got back."

DiGrassio shook his head. "I wish I could do something like that, but I have a brown thumb."

A large monarch fluttered up against the window, winking with its wings before veering back toward a clump of robust cosmos.

"Oh, it's easy," Mary Grace said. "You just need the right fertilizer. Another cookie, detective?"

Allergies

Doree Weller

Allen sneezed and reached for the bottle of allergy medication. "I hate spring." He fumbled with the cap and sniffed.

"Hey, you ever hear about why people say 'Bless you' when you sneeze?" Donny asked.

"Don't know. Don't care." Allen got the lid off and tilted the bottle to drop a capsule into his hand.

"Hey, stop a second." Donny put his hand out and Allen paused. "Everything stops when you sneeze. Your heart, your brain, everything. So, supposedly the devil can possess you. If someone says 'Bless you,' it drives the devil out."

"Fascinating. What's your point?"

"Let's try it out. Let's go sit outside in the field and have you sneeze for awhile, see what happens."

Allen rolled his eyes and grabbed his soda, taking a long swig to drive the tickle out of his throat. He blew his nose and wiped his watery eyes. "You have the dumbest ideas."

"Oh, come on. Unless you're scared?"

Allen sighed, knowing that once Donny had an idea, he wouldn't let it rest until he was satisfied. "Fine," he agreed.

The boys trooped out to the field, Allen with his soda and box of tissues, Donny with the mouth that never rested.

"What was it like being in Alabama?" Donny asked.

"It was boring. My grandparents are like 150 years old and eat all kinds of weird stuff."

"So, you feel the devil in you yet?"

Allen sneezed again and eyed a daffodil. He wiped his nose. "No devil. Ready to go back in now?"

"Just a little bit longer."

"Are you trying to kill me?"

Donny laughed. "No." He grabbed Allen's soda and took a sip. He rubbed his lips and sneezed.

"Uh oh, sounds like the devil's looking at you, too," Allen commented.

"I feel kind of weird." Donny took another sip of soda. "Your soda tastes weird."

Allen shrugged.

Donny grabbed his throat and dropped the soda on the ground, foam leaking into the weeds. "Can't breathe. My epi pen is in the house."

"What's going on?" Allen asked. "You okay?"

"Hurry."

Allen ran into the house as fast as he could, wheezing. When he got inside, he grabbed another soda and dropped another handful of peanuts in the can. It was something he picked up in Alabama, and he liked it. He took a long swig, then grabbed Donny's back-pack and threw everything on the floor, as if he had gone through it in a hurry. He found the epi pen in the front pocket, and tucked it into his jeans before running back to Donny.

Donny lay on his side, an unfortunate shade of blue. "What do I do with this?" Allen asked, but Donny was beyond answering. Allen nudged Donny with his toe, but Donny didn't react. Allen commented quietly, "I've had allergies all my life. This wasn't my first sneeze."

Allen smiled, and pulled out his phone to dial 911.

Spring Showers

Stephanie L. Morrell

Dark and gloomy clouds blocked out the sunlight for days and it seemed the weekend would be no different. Sam's mood was affected by the constant bad weather and it altered his personality.

"When will this spring rainstorm end?" He looked to his wife for comfort.

"Not soon enough." Sara handed him a cup of coffee. "It's Saturday so why don't we take Joey to the movies?"

"I'm not really up to it."

"Come on, Sam. Joey's been stuck in this house for days and he's only six years old. Surely you can get yourself together long enough to cheer him up with a trip to the movies."

"I'm just not in the mood for a theater full of noisy kids and shushing parents."

"Fine," her brown eyes darkened. "I'll take him."

Sam took his coffee outside and drops of rainwater *plunk, plunk, plunked* into it.

"When the hell will we get some sun around here?" He snatched up the soggy plastic bag containing the morning paper and gulped down his drink.

***

Sara and Joey went off to the movies while Sam stayed home and did some work around the house. After a couple of hours, he was hit with a wave of nausea followed by violent fits of vomiting. What he spewed into the toilet was muddy-green in color and unlike anything he had ingested. He made his way to the kitchen for some soda and crackers to settle his stomach and noticed the empty coffee cup in the sink. The inside of it was very much altered from this morning. The white color inside had turned a greenish-brown and tiny yellow insects were squirming around at the bottom.

"What the hell?"

Sam noticed the discoloration in the cup matched the color of his vomit and the thought made him gag. He ran into the bathroom for another bout of sickness and this time he studied his retching more closely. It was an exact match to the contents inside of his coffee cup. On closer examination, he noticed there were tiny yellow spots peppered throughout and the spots appeared to be moving.

"Are those bugs?" He spoke loudly. "Oh, God. Those freakin' things are inside me."

The thought of those yellow insects squirming around inside of him lead Sam to another round of aggressive vomiting.

"What was in that rain water?"

Sam believed those tiny yellow insects were crawling around inside of his stomach and making their way up into his esophagus. He called Sara but her phone was switched off for the movie. The idea of going to the hospital frightened Sam. He wanted to get rid of whatever was inside his body; however, the thought of being diagnosed with some lethal bacteria was more than he could stand. If the rainwater contaminated Sam's system, he wanted to treat the problem on his own.

"All that I have to do is clear my body of this shit and I will be fine."

Sam drank a large glass of water from the fridge and then jammed a toothbrush down his throat. He shoved it into his esophagus until the gag reflex took hold. Soon, he was vomiting profusely and the consistency remained the same. Worse still, the number of insects was in abundance. Sam could not fathom the idea that any liquid remained in his system. A combination of depression, fluid loss and fear tainted his thoughts. The solution he considered next was irrational at best, but he was certain it would work. He made a mixture of Jack Daniels and a bit of liquid drain cleaner to kill off the bugs.

"This will do it." His face was pale and swollen from excessive vomiting and broken blood vessels peppered the flesh around his eyes. "The Jack will get me drunk while the drain cleaner kills off the bugs."

Sam ingested the drink and vomited until his system was clear. A wide smile spread across his lips as he slipped into unconsciousness.

***

Sara and Joey returned home to find Sam's lifeless body on the bathroom floor. The frozen smile on his face made the scene more grotesque and a terrible thing for his family to observe.

The coroner ruled his death a suicide as there was nothing in his system but alcohol and poison.

Sara returned from the hospital, put Joey to bed, and then noticed Sam's dirty coffee cup. It was perfectly white inside with a tiny coffee stain along the rim and the sight of it made her weep.

Dew on their Blades

D.G. Sutter

Where there should have been, dampened, a patch of brown earth, the ground lay bare—beyond a doubt, dry—surrounded by thick green grass, grown high. Allen could not quite figure it out. The night had brought rain, in plentiful bouts, and seeds he had sown laid fresh in the spot, had washed with the rain and left clear with drought.

Day after day, he left seeds piled high, hoping that some would take root and would rise. Yet the grass never grew, the seeds floated away, and the promise of life from the ground escaped.

A fat, well-fed robin flew down from its perch and pecked at the ground for a fat, stringy worm. When none could be found, the bird flew away, another let down on a gentle spring day.

Around the dry patch, blades glistened with dew. He avoided them carefully, to replace old dirt with new. Two feet he dug down until he hit rock, then heaved out the clumps and the heaps, and stopped.

The bag he fetched was heavy indeed, slung on his shoulder, carried to the patch. When Allen reached the hole, he dropped to his knee and peered in, aghast.

The hole was filled with small life, it writhed and it stared; through tiny eyes, beady and black. They crawled by their arms and their legs dragged behind, and they screamed "Feed us, father!" heads arched on their spines.

Their tiny heads were covered with hair, and they fought with each other for room and for air. Allen grasped his shovel in two shaky hands, raised it high above his head, and dropped with despair. Over and over the tool connected with rock, till the movement ceased inside the small plot.

The man filled the hole with soil to the top. He planted no more seed, nor watered the ground. He knew he would raise no life from the grave; it was not meant to be, it'd always been dead.

Let's Go, Warlocks!

Dan Larnerd

Since Gabby pulled out of the gas station, the bus had been following her. It loomed like a monster over her small car with its wide grill and headlights filling her rearview mirror.

The sun had just dipped below the horizon, casting a golden hue across the darkening sky. Gabby eyed the empty fields nervously as the bus tailgated close behind. On both sides of the highway, there was nothing but plowed farmlands that were just showing the first signs of the spring crop. Up ahead, there was just more and more absolute nothing.

"Come on, buddy," Gabby said nervously. "There's enough highway for the both of us."

Suddenly, the bus lunged around her car into the passing lane. It was an older style from the late sixties with a sleek front end and curved edges. It seemed so massive as it towered beside Gabby's car.

A large logo caught Gabby's attention on the side of the van. The wizard on the logo had a lecherous grin that made her skin crawl. He wore a pointed wizard hat covered with stars but with a baseball cap's brim. His long, flowing beard draped down to his knees. In his gloved-hands was a baseball bat with a star at the end like it was a magic wand.

Stretching across the length of the bus was a banner proclaiming: 'Let's Go Warlocks! Good Luck at Spring Training!'

Sneering from the windows were the faces of young men. It was like looking into a bullpen at the ballpark. They were all wearing purple baseball caps and some were tapping bats on the glass. Driving themselves into a frenzy, they were hooting at Gabby and banging on the windows.

Wide-eyed, Gabby took her foot off the accelerator slowing the car. The bus matched her speed and keep along side of her.

"Okay. I'm officially weirded out now," Gabby said to herself.

Shaking, Gabby reached over to her purse on the passenger's

seat. She reached in and grabbed her cell phone. Suddenly, something cracked the driver's side window. Startled, Gabby dropped her phone.

Baseballs began to rain down on the hood and bounced into the windshield. Gabby was showered in broken glass. Screaming, she slammed on the brake pedal and twisted the wheel, causing the car to skid.

She screamed again as her car left the highway. It flipped and twisted in midair. With a loud crunch, it came crashing down in the gutter. The bus hissed to a stop as the car came to rest on its top. For Gabby, the world went from red to black.

As she regained consciousness, Gabby could hear muffled voices. A sharp pain in her side shot pain through her body. In her mouth, she could taste blood and her throat was dry. Her head was swimming in a fog of pain and confusion.

The voices came into focus as her head cleared. The ballplayers from the bus surrounded her and were singing *Take Me Out to the Ballgame* slow and deliberately like a funeral dirge.

Overhead, stadium lights flared into her eyes. Empty bleachers were all around her. Gabby realized her head was on home plate. She struggled to move but was tied to the ground.

When the song came to an end, a pot-bellied manager with gray hair walked out to the pitcher's mound. The players cheered until the old man put up his hand. The players went silent and took off their caps.

"Boys," the manager said. "As we start spring training, I want you all to remember that a winning season takes hard work and it also takes… sacrifice!"

Cheers went up as the manager walked over to Gabby and knelt beside her in the batter's box. The players huddled around, as the manager put on a catcher's mitt. He gently placed his gloved hand on her forehead.

The manager looked to the sky and said solemnly, "Oh, Lords of the Infield and Masters of the Outfield! We remember the ancient traditions of the great game when it was played with a femur and skull. Bless us with stolen bases and turn our foul balls fair. Cause our enemies to error and blind the umpires to our intrigue. In the name of the great ones: Mantle, Ruth and Cobb, we offer you this flesh. Let this sacrifice give us victory on the way to the pennant."

“Bring out Wally!” shouted a player with a bushy mustache.

“Wally!” another agreed.

The manager left Gabby’s side and waved someone over. The scoreboard in the outfield came alive. Its lights flashed as if it was possessed. Gabby twisted her head to see who was approaching.

Wally was the wizard mascot Gabby had seen painted on the side of the bus. The huge plush head made him look sinister and demonic. His giant styrofoam eyes looked cold and empty.

The mascot started taking swings with a bat loaded down with batting doughnuts. He tapped his bat against his cleats and the team went wild. Then, as a full moon hung above, Wally called his shot by pointing to right field.

“No… Don’t do this,” Gabby cried.

The mascot loamed over Gabby with his bat raised above his head. The team began to chant.

“Swing, batter, batter. Swing.”

Renewal

Chad McKee

Kim gazed down at the streets below, a tremble of excitement electrifying her body. She didn't let herself make a sound though, but peered silently through the trees high on the hill in case anyone recognized her.

Someone would. Someone always did.

But should she worry? The story was true! Her own eyes drank in the tranquility. The town was not large—a village, really, with the typical sort of late colonial architecture of New England, a Georgian church in the tiny town square. Smartly cut grass, a new coat of paint on the street lamps. Picket fences. Like a postcard!

And the people? They had sparkling eyes like polished silver. There was happiness in them. The binoculars helped, of course, but it was in their walk, too. No matter how they ambled along, young or old, it was with confidence. Right on the streets, not from behind darkened windows like she had been for so long.

But the trees were what really caught her eye. Long, beautiful rows of Cherries and Magnolias, just in bloom now as the Winter frosts were cast off and the spring renewal began. It was this fortress of trees that barricaded the little town from the rest of the world, made it livable for its tiny population. She had heard, that in winter, the snows and the town's general remoteness made it nearly impossible to find. That's why she had waited, had spent the last three months in that stinking hole in South Boston, biding her time.

It was a bittersweet feeling, having run so long and finally finding her destination. She could see herself strolling down the main street, greeting her neighbors and buying cakes from the bakery and, perhaps, chatting with the minister as she left the Sunday Service. A normal life. No more police, no more running. No more hiding her face.

Absently, Kim rubbed the skin of her cheeks, the crest of her eyebrow. She thought she was attractive. Certainly, many had told her so—that was part of the reason she had been running for years. One too many had brought her into bed against her will and she had cut them where the most damage could be done. You couldn't believe how the blood could pump from that area.

The softness of her skin suddenly repulsed her; the eloquence of her cheekbones mocked her. Why couldn't she just be ugly? That would have made things so much easier.

They wouldn't take her this way. That's what the woman in the hospital had told her once. She couldn't be perfect and expect to fit in. Kim had believed it, seeing the woman's body, thickly contorted with massive tumors, a victim of Proteus Syndrome.

And it was true; she could see it even from her perch high above the village. The awkward gait of the grocer with a club foot. A mailman with one arm. A little boy skipping along the sidewalk with a face split by a severe cleft pallet. A woman missing a jaw. A minister who preached from a wheelchair, his legs gone all together.

Kim had been prepared for this, though. She unzipped her backpack and brought out the bottle—what was left of it. She had broken it a mile away, when she saw the beautiful line of trees making a perimeter around the town. She said to herself: I can sew, I can cook, I can sell shoes, and I can sing a lovely alto in the church choir. This was her litany of self worth, what she could offer the town. She repeated it five times in a whisper, hoping that it was enough.

But now, she was too perfect. Not a blemish on her body, save a few freckles and a facial mole that most called a "beauty mark."

She didn't want it anymore, nor the soft flesh of her face. She had been hiding it for almost a decade—what use was it to her? She could lose herself here. Nobody would find her. Nobody. It had taken her two years and she had been told where to go.

Almost. One more thing to endure. She got out a bottle of alcohol and her needle and thread. She couldn't do much about the blood loss, but she had plenty of sugary food—cookies, donuts, Little Debbie's. She hoped to stave off any faintness with those.

She selected the sharpest looking piece of bottle. Despite its savageness, she was not really afraid. Still, she kept her breaths as even as she could and tried to control her heartbeat. It would be worth it, this final process of transformation. A renewal, just like the blooming of the trees in the spring. She would be protected. She did gag herself with a bit of rag, though.

This was going to hurt. This was going to leave a scar.

Spring Clean Out

Sean O'Connor

Old Mrs. Rosemary put the newspaper down and sighed. Out the window, she could see the spring blossoms shinning in her garden, as though she'd gone and painted them in bright colors over night.

Well, it's that time of year, she thought, using her old arms to lever herself off the couch. T*ime to do the spring clean out*.

Truth was, she'd been putting it off for days, ever since she saw the first signs of colors from her flowers in the front garden, actually. It just seemed that she accumulated more and more junk every year, and that cleaning it all up come spring was becoming more and more of a tedious chore.

Still, it had to be done, and no one else was going to do it. She just had to get off her old backside and get her hands dirty, like she always had.

Mrs. Rosemary, a seventy-two year old Senior Citizens member, started in her basement, where she'd put old records during the year which were of no use now that she had the fancy new thing called a CD player.

"Now, what am I to do with these?" she said, caressing a couple of the records in her arm. She had one black garbage bag for the bin, another garbage bag which would go to the local second hand shop, and a box for things she couldn't bear to part with. She'd gather all those up at the end of the clean out and place them neatly in the attic.

Mrs. Rosemary dug into her work, using those hands which had stitched quilts for almost fifty-five years now, to gather up the junk, placing them into separate spots, sneezing as dust mites reached her nose.

She finished with the basement and got started with the lounge room.

"I don't need those magazines anymore," she said, speaking to herself and throwing out her collection of Garden Monthly magazines. She moved to the kitchen, collecting old Tupperware containers and binning them, fixing the jars of jam and marmalade in the pantry, throwing out that out-of-date can of spaghetti.

Finally, having done the first floor and the second floor—including her messy bedroom which had looked like a pack of wild dogs had rummaged through it before she got there—she reached the attic.

She carefully stepped up the ladder, minding her old frail legs. She pulled the string of the trapdoor then popped her head through.

Staring back at her were copious amounts of dead bodies. Some had been dismembered, their cold, marble eyes looking at her in horror, frozen in the bleak moment of death. Some were so chopped to pieces it was really hard to tell where the eyes were; there were severed legs strewn about, one up against the old mirror, smearing old dry blood on it. Some of the bodies had distinct axe blade marks cut deep into them, the guts on one body sifting out from the excavation. The smell was horrid; like walking into a disused greenhouse, all the flowers rotten and dead, their stench brain numbing.

She covered her nose.

"Now I forgot all about those," she said in a nasally voice, looking at her attic is disgust, home to a dozen or so mutilated bodies. "This is going to take me all spring to clean."

She carefully went back down the steps, made her way to her garage where she had the pickaxe hanging off the wall, red crusted blood still stuck to its blade.

"Where is it, where is it?" she muttered. Then she saw the mop and bucket. "That's what I'm looking for," she said swiping it up. She stopped before she left the garage. "I'll probably be needing a few of these too," she said, heading back to grab five or six of the large black garbage bags she'd been using to store things.

Old Mrs. Rosemary made her way back up to the attic.

"I'll have to be more careful next time," she said once there, lifting a severed head by the hair and dumping it into the garbage bag. "Have to remember not to make such a mess."

Allergy Season

Sean Graham

The radio crackled on the kitchen table. A man's voice emanated from the speakers, raspy and dry. He coughed. "This is WJGK, government radio...." He went on to the day's pollen count, the only thing anybody really cared about besides a cure. "...so stay indoors," the disc jockey finished.

"And try not to breathe," Aaron said to no one. He was alone downstairs in their suburban home. His wife, Ann, was in bed upstairs. Outside, a thick fog of allergens floated through the air, shrouding the world in a yellow-white haze. Across the street, over his waist-high grass, he watched a car smolder. Mowing had become impossible months ago; the idea of maintaining a lawn was laughable now, and he had been concerned the fire might spread, but it hadn't. A dead dog lay in the street, its body covered in pollen. Half a dozen red blossoms grew from its carcass.

The government DJ moved on to the death toll: "...nationwide, three hundred more have perished since Sunday. Rossweed pollen, the likely cause of death...." Aaron flipped the power switch and the static-laced voice vanished. The rest would be a repeat of the previous months.

He scratched under the surgeon's mask that never left his face and then ran his fingers along the window. Outside, the microscopic particles followed his fingers. He pressed his palm against the glass and removed it. The pollen left a detailed mirror impression of his hand on the glass, right down to the love line in his palm. Sentient and aggressive allergen, he recalled from early news broadcasts, from a time when there was an actual media and more mattered in life than the pollen count. For the thousandth time that morning, he checked the wet rags that lined the windows and doors.

A thud sounded overhead.

Aaron left the window and walked upstairs, his feet dropping like dumbbells, the edges of his vision running black. From the top of the stairs, he could see the master bedroom and the painter's tarp taped over the doorway, a film of yellow pollen covering the inside.

Through the pollen, behind the frosted sheet of plastic he could see the end of the bed he once shared with his wife and the untouched cases of water and canned goods he had forced her to keep.

For the first few days after Ann began coughing, they would lean against the wall near the covered doorway and talk to each other. Mostly fun stuff: embarrassing moments, old friends, family, funny movies. One night, Ann rubbed a clear spot in the tarp and pressed a bloodshot eye to it and they watched their honeymoon DVD for hours on repeat. The last time they spoke, she could barely breathe. He had said he loved her and they pressed their hands against the plastic and she tried to respond, but could only manage a gurgling wet sound that was too much for Aaron to bear. He had left her there that day as she had asked him to do when the end was clear, and he had not gone back upstairs since.

A colorless hand lay across the floor near the door and he had to force his steps forward. The smell of feces and bitter body odor hung in the air. Through the tarp, he saw the red blossom growing from Ann's hand, a gift offered up to whoever should find her lifeless body. The roots sprouted from her pale flesh like venous extensions.

Moving closer, stretching the tarp inward like a baby's foot testing the boundaries of his mother's womb, the plastic molding to the contours of his face, Aaron angled to see more of his wife. Tears fell. The pollen followed the curves of his face forming a yellow, powdered skull on the inside of the plastic. Ann's face, pointed to the ceiling, was pale and bloated. Mercifully, her eyes were swollen shut. Burst blood vessels crisscrossed her skin in constellation lines. A red blossom sat in her mouth.

Aaron leaned further, the plastic pulled, the tape popped slightly but held. He wanted to kiss her, caress her, take the gift from her hand. Why had he left her? What was the point of going on at all and without her, trapped alone in his living room as the world crumbled against the heel of an antigen? He thought of her final moments; suffocating, the pollen filling her lungs, the seedlings sprouting in her organs, her solitude and the loneliness she must have felt, the abandonment.

"Ann." He pushed the tarp and the tape gave way. Immediately, yellow-white pollen washed over him. It pulled at him, sought his mouth, his nose. Aaron sat next to his wife and pulled her into his lap and kissed her over the flower in her mouth. It was sweet tasting, then bitter, its petals shifting around his tongue.

He lay beside her, inhaled deeply and waited for the coughing to start.

April Showers

E.J. Tett

She left her book on the arm of the chair and got up to go and peer out of the window. It was raining again, the daffodils in her garden were taking a beating from the downpour and she pursed her lips.

It's because of the jet stream moving north. She could hear his voice in her head explaining the weather to her. *It's a phenomenon*, he would say. *And you thought April Showers was just an expression.*

She hadn't given it that much thought. It was only the weather; it always seemed to rain in the springtime in this damn country.

Tapping her fingers on the windowsill, she peered further into the garden. *At least the rain stops them*, she thought. *They don't like the rain…*

She chewed her lip, wondering whether to go out now. She needed food but would it carry on raining long enough for her to get it?

Come on, his voice again, *we can't hide in here forever*!

He'd always been brave. They had laughed and ran to the car together, driven down the deserted streets and then raced around the empty shops, filling their cart before hurrying back to the car again. They had been safe that time, they hadn't seen any of *them…*

"Can't," she muttered, moving away from the window. She returned to her chair and picked up the book. Her hands trembled a little now and her eyes constantly flicked back to the window and then to the front door.

"You're safe," she told herself.

We're safe! He had said. *We've survived this long, haven't we? Me and you like this. It's meant to be*!

A sob caught in her throat and she looked up from her book towards the window again. Rain hammered against the glass and she took comfort from that.

They don't like the rain, she reminded herself. She took a deep, steadying breath and put her book down again. She went into the kitchen and sorted through the fridge and the cupboards, seeing exactly how much food she had left.

"You need food," she said aloud, shaking her hands by her side to try and get rid of the nervous energy. "Go and get it. Now."

Before she could think herself out of it, she was moving back through the house, grabbing her car keys from the coffee table and the pistol she kept under her pillow. She checked that the weapon was loaded and then went back into the kitchen to get a knife as a back-up weapon.

Always carry a knife, he said. *Promise me*?

"I promise," she muttered, tucking the blade carefully through her belt. She went to look out of the window again. It was still raining and the daffodils were still getting a pounding.

She opened up the front door and ran to the car, unlocking it and then diving inside before locking the door again. She sat in the driving seat and shivered.

It's cold and wet and miserable in your country! She remembered yelling it at him. All she had wanted to do was go home.

He had just laughed. *Get used to it*.

The windshield wipers squeaked across the glass and she wondered if they needed replacing. "Does it matter?" she asked herself. She put the car into gear and moved off.

Overhead, the sky was starting to clear and the spots of rain on her windscreen became fewer and fewer. The squeaking was getting worse as the rubber dried out. She let out a slow breath between her lips and prayed for the rain.

When sun broke through the clouds, she cursed.

Don't panic, just turn the car around and go home. Remembering his voice helped and she turned the car in the road. Her heart hammered in her chest. Everything was too quiet now the rain had stopped.

"They're coming," she sobbed, though she couldn't see anything yet. She glanced in her rear view mirror and then back at the road.

She slammed on her brakes.

The creature was standing in the middle of the road, inches from the front of her car. Blood ran in rivulets down its face as she fumbled for her pistol.

A shadow passed overhead and the sun disappeared once more behind a cloud. *April showers*, she thought, and laughed hysterically as it began to rain again.

The creature screamed and writhed in sudden pain and she put her foot to the floor and swerved around it, not daring to look back.

Once she reached her house, she bolted from the car, locking it with a press of a button. It was still raining as she reached her front door, though she stopped suddenly and stood there, staring.

The front door was open. Just a crack. But it was open. She realized she'd been holding her breath and she let it out now raggedly.

Did I leave it open? She couldn't remember. She held the pistol tight and pushed the door open.

He was sitting on the sofa reading her book. Only it wasn't him anymore. He was like all the others now. When he turned his head to look at her she saw the blood run down his face.

"Oh, God," she choked. Her hands trembled and she couldn't quite bring herself to pull the trigger as he got up and approached her. She stood there and let him take the gun from her.

She stepped back out into the rain and he smiled a bloody smile before closing the door on her. The clouds drifted apart and the sun warmed her face.

She heard footsteps behind her. *Always carry a knife*, he had said. And she did.

Tilling

Matthew Marovich

He paused for a moment to arch his spine and was rewarded with a series of stress-releasing pops. His shoulders and back ached from honest work, hands dirty from his toils on the land. He could feel the sun on his forearms and was thankful for the wide straw hat. The last thing he needed was cancer and the hat made sun block on his face unnecessary, a good thing because he *hated* sun block on his face.

It's always tough work tilling the fields and he wasn't getting any younger. The farmer frowned as he looked across the field of freshly upturned earth, the four scarecrows on their crosses. Soon, he'd be too old for this.

"But not this year," he said to himself.

He walked over to his newest scarecrow and smiled up at his handiwork. The stitching on this one had been particularly skillful, the black thread showing up nicely against the pale face. A ratty straw hat over the head kept the sun off and he'd dressed it in some of his old, threadbare clothes. The other three were similarly dressed; three stood at the end of long rows of freshly tilled earth while the fourth stood above an open trench about six feet long.

Well, he remarked wryly to himself, ignoring the moans coming from above him, *it was time to get to work.*

From the wheelbarrow next to the trench, he hefted a body. It'd belonged to a young man, loud, brash, disrespectful. The young man and his friends had come down the farmer's road in two sports cars, racing each other. They must have thought it was one of several abandoned roads running through the countryside, so it had probably been a surprise when they shot around a bend and the lead car had rammed one of his prize dairy cows. The impact destroyed the car, sent it spinning off to land upside-down in a ditch, and, worse, it had killed his cow. The farmer's milk cows were some of the best producers in the county; it was a loss that was difficult to take, especially given the callous, irresponsible way it happened.

Those from the second car showed up asking for help but the

farmer hadn't been sure what help they expected. He frowned as he thought about how they had pleaded, the rage that'd come over him when he learned what happened. His shotgun had killed the one he was lifting out of the wheelbarrow. Another two shells had taken out the tires on their remaining car before they could drive away. The other three scattered and he hunted them across his property; two he killed with his pitchfork, the last he caught up with outside the wreck, killing her with his bare hands as he choked the life from her from behind. Four of their friends were still in the overturned car, a mixture of hurt and unconscious, and he'd taken care of them too.

They might've killed his cow, and they'd never replace it, but they'd pay him back one way or the other.

He dumped the body into the trench face up. The shotgun blast had blown a hole in the boy's chest and his face was locked in a mask of shock and pain. From inside his overalls, the farmer took a long, thick-bladed knife that gleamed as clean and as sharp as a surgeon's scalpel. He always looked after his tools.

With a long, easy stroke be split the body from just below the chin all the way to his short hairs. Years of farm labor had given him strength and he pulled the wound open wide, tearing the flesh and muscle back. Once that was done he went back to wheelbarrow and collected a burlap sack. From it he pulled out a handful of seeds, some of which clung to him, stuck in the clotting blood covering his hands and arms. With a few practiced shakes of his wrist, he scattered seeds into the slit. By the time he was done filling in the furrow in the earth and patting the dirt flat and smooth, he was really considering buying one of those jacuzzi things; his body just *ached.*

The farmer looked across his fields at all the four rows of dirt, each topped with a scarecrow on a cross, arms widely outspread. Some still shook and moaned from having been freshly mounted. From under the stitched shut lids of the scarecrow before him, tears slowly rolled over hollow, dusty cheeks, collecting along the jaw, before falling to the thirsty dirt below.

"You be good now," he said, patting the scarecrow on the hip. "I don't want to see a single crow on these fields."

The farmer walked back towards his farmhouse past fields with even rows, each ending with their own scarecrow, some little more than sagging, desiccated flesh and bone. He'd worked his farm for years, and he was looking forward to a shower to relax his muscles.

A just reward, he thought, for his hard work tilling the fields.

The Time of Renewal

Angela Alsaleem

None of the children in Gertrude's town questioned why she paid $10 per tooth for those who brought them. The parents assumed she simply enjoyed the company, having gone to her estate when they were young for the same reason. Besides, she was harmless.

Gertrude rolled a tooth between her fingers as she walked toward her private cemetery, breathing in the air. Not a cloud in the sky.

Typically the first day of spring marked her favorite time of year, but this spring would be the last one with him. Trying to slough off the disappointment, she reminded herself that she was grateful, dammit! 50 springs was better than nothing. The mile hike from the house to the graves wore on her old body, but she grinned through the pain.

She had 91 teeth. One for every day of spring. One for every day she could take back from death and be with Thomas again, now 50 years dead.

The cemetery came into view. The tombstones leaned like crooked teeth. Out of the generations buried here, only Thomas's body interested her.

It was the time of renewal, after all. When she'd made the bargain at age 30, she thought she'd die before she ran out of time, death allowing her eternity with her beloved. Now she knew better. Looking at Thomas's tombstone, she wondered how much longer she'd have to live without his touch once this spring ended, wondered if that was her curse, to live forever, alone.

She crouched over the grave, the only grave for her. Gertrude caressed the marble, traced her finger over the epitaph, her withered hand trembling. With the sleeve of her robe, she wiped off the dirt. A tear fell as she forced another smile.

"I've come back again, Thomas, my love," she whispered. After clearing the leaves, she shoved her finger into the earth then placed the tooth inside. Once she finished covering it, she stood back and unwrapped her robe, letting it pool around her feet.

Fog rolled in and enveloped her trembling body, moisture condensing on her wrinkled skin. Her gray hair fell to her waist as she lifted her arms over her head and turned her face toward the sky, reciting her incantation. Clouds gathered, as they always did. Thunder shook the ground, rain poured, soaking her. She shivered and wrapped her arms around her frail body, running her fingers over her protruding ribs, her thin flesh.

When the ground opened at her feet, Gertrude laughed, the same laugh from her youth, a laugh meant only for Thomas. The mud squished between her toes as she bounced and clapped. She watched the fissure expand, and straddled it, letting the crack run between her legs.

Soon, her beloved Thomas would rise. Soon, he would hold her, warm, young, renewed. He'd kiss her face, tell her death was cruel to keep them apart. He'd pet her hair and say she was beautiful, no matter her age. Then, at nightfall, she'd have to leave him to repeat the process the next dawn. One more tooth. One more day. Anger burned her belly at the injustice of death. She clenched her fists and forced another smile. She would take what she could.

A clawed hand shot up from the earth.

She tripped in her haste to get away from the opening. Pain flared in her hip as she hit the ground.

Another clawed hand shot out. The thing pushed itself up and grinned at her.

"But it's not time," she shouted at the demon. "Where's Thomas?" She tried to back away, feet squelching in the mud, but she slid forward as the ground tilted and the creature crawled toward her.

It laughed.

"I get one more spring with him," she shouted. "We had a deal."

It laid down on top of her, grinding its pelvis into her. Her hip screamed.

"I have all the teeth I need to keep you, now." the demon said.

Gertrude flopped onto her stomach and clawed at the muck, the demon's hot breath on her neck, but to no avail. The two of them slid into the fissure together, and the sludge fell in around them. The creature wrapped its burning arms around her and stroked her hair as mud filled her mouth.

"My love," it whispered and kissed her face, laughing.

To keep her? She finally understood. Thomas died 50 years ago. There was no renewal from death.

"You're so beautiful," it cooed. "And you're all mine."

Springtime Slaughter

Nick Medina

The Bible says that there's a time to be born and a time to die; a time to plant, and a time to pluck up that which is planted; a time to kill, and a time to heal. The complete psalm—found in Ecclesiastes—makes everything sound so simple, so futile. And while I've lived my life according to that string of sacred words, I've found that life and living requires much more than a series of opposing events; nothing is simple, nothing is futile.

To live is to labor. To survive is to struggle. If I hadn't spent the previous spring and the subsequent summer scraping together the slags who'd sought to feast on me, I'd have had nothing to feast on myself. It's always been that way. I work my fingers to the bone scraping meat off the bone all through the warm weather months so that when winter comes I can hunker down with a belly that'll stay full until the warm rays of spring come to melt the unsightly snow away.

It's almost all gone now: the meat and the snow. Spring moved in and winter hit the road at precisely midnight the day before. Now, all that remains of the icy crystals that fell from the sky so fiercely during the frigid, dark days of January and February are glistening mounds that will take hours to melt completely.

Gazing through my bedroom window, I watch the rivulets of water cascade down the sides of the disappearing snow mounds. The snow itself is mushy and gray and covered with specks of dirt. The mound closest to me is marked with tracks. I recognize the soggy imprints as the impressions left by the soles of my winter boots. If ever I had spotted the imprints of some foreign footwear, I would have hit the ground running for fear of my secret being broadcast beyond my humble backyard. But for now, my secret is safe. And I intend on keeping it that way.

Knowing the struggle I'll face come nightfall, however, I can't help but think that maybe I'm getting too old for this. My face isn't as youthful as it once was. My eyes aren't as bright. My teeth aren't as white. Strip the dye from my hair and you'll find an obscene amount of gray. Year in and year out, season after season, I feel that I'm losing my looks. With every wrinkle that mars my face and every extra pound that clings to my failing frame, I know I'm coming closer to retirement. And then I'll starve for sure.

But, at the moment, that's too much to ponder; too much to fret. I'd much rather sit here by the window watching the snow mounds grow smaller and smaller while the sun climbs higher in the sky. There's a patch of grass by the fence at the end of the yard where the snow wasn't so deep. Unlike the lush, lance-shaped leaves of the tulips sprouting out of the ground in the flower beds, the grass is brown. It won't be green for another week or two.

While Mother Nature may take her sweet time covering winter's palette with spring's abundance of vivid and vibrant shades, I color my skin to create the illusion of youth. My cheeks are bronzed. My eyelids are blue. My lips are as red as the tulips that haven't yet bloomed. And if all goes as planned, my lips won't be all that's red once the night is through.

Digging through my closet, searching for the clothes I haven't worn since autumn put an end to my comfortable nights trolling the boulevard beneath the light of the summer's moon, I hear a dog bark followed by a scream. For an instant, I think that my secret's been discovered, but, when I look outside again, I see that there's nothing to fear. The scream turns into a giggle and the dog goes on barking. Somewhere down the street the neighbor's kids are playing with what's left of their snow before it's gone for good.

Breathing easier, I sit once again. My fishnets in one hand and my stilettos in the other, I remind myself to target the smaller ones; the big johns are so much harder to carry home, even though, with all their fat, they do tend to taste so much better.

Wiping some spit on the toe of my left high heel to remove a dried speck of blood, I gaze out the window once again. My snow mounds are nearly gone. And in their absence, I see all that remains of my winter feast: a single severed hand poking through the snow, its forefinger bent as though beckoning me out into the sun.

And it's true, I must get going. My stock needs replenishing and winter will be here before I know it. To everything, there is a season.

The Springing of Him

Paul DeCirce

Jim met Beth at the garden by the bridge, the place her husband died. Drove off the bridge, broke the flimsy wooden guardrails, and crashed down into the small creek below. The hood was crushed flat; the body, oddly, was never found.

The first shivering flowers of spring were popping from the cold dirt, their pale color transparent in the still harsh winds. They slumped, beaten from the last rain, held down by the dew. When Jim arrived, the first rays of morning sun were peeking through the trees lining the park. He looked up to the bridge, counted maybe a hundred feet to the rocky waters below. *A long fall*, Jim thought, sipping his coffee. He set Beth's cup at the edge of the green bench.

Jim had comforted her in the year since. He was there for her; a reassuring hand for her shoulder, to brush away the hair stuck to her moist eyes, to wipe away those tears. She trusted him, she was even learning to love him. And, most importantly, she had no idea.

Her marriage had been short; Jim met the happy couple when they'd first tied the knot. Less than two years before his unfortunate accident. The husband had been on his way home from work and took the park as a shortcut. The police claimed he must have been speeding along real good to burst through the rails like that.

Then again, Jim thought, brushing his lap as a drop of coffee spilled there, *the police claimed a lot*.

They claimed the man must have lived. There was no accounting for the missing body, otherwise. He'd be found, they said at first, probably in a hospital or wandering the streets with a concussion. Three days, then a week passed for Beth. Jim was there for her then, rushing to her side.

Jim had been an office associate of his. He met Beth at a function; her husband had brought her to dine. He'd been knocked asunder by her beauty that night.

Three days turned into three weeks, three months. He never turned up. No hospitals, no reports of him on the streets. Jim helped her face the reality: it had all been an elaborate plan for him to abandon her. He showed Beth the denial of her questions; then he convinced her.

He isn't coming back.

And now, the same day one year later, he watched Beth walking up the path. Jim set down his coffee and stood when he saw her. She had her arms around herself, and she walked slowly. Her long hair waved around her red windbreaker, her clear eyes covered with shades. He remembered the jackets had been matching; a gift from the husband before he'd left.

"Hey," she said, her mouth quivering. She reached for him, needing the comfort. He soothed her, kissed her hair.

"Come on, sit down," he said. "Got this for you."

"Thanks," she said, taking the cup and holding it with both hands.

"Maybe this was too soon?" Jim said.

"No, no, it's good." She regarded the coffee cup. "You've been so good to me, you know that?"

He played coy. "Those daisies are beautiful, aren't they?" He asked, motioning toward the garden bed. Their tender petals clutched to one another. Hundreds of them, lining the bed, were beginning to stand proud from the steady sunshine. Their fellows in the community garden were showing their colors as well: peonies, tulips, and heather. The yellow daisy florets blinked at her, and she stood to get a better look.

"You know," he said as she walked across the narrow stone path, "today symbolizes a new beginning, a time for you to spread your wings."

She didn't hear him. She was curious about the flowers; they were bending in unison against the wind. Their tender petals craned their thin stems toward her as she bent to brush her hand across them. Jim sat frowning, looked at the coffee he'd bought her, its lid off. Getting cold.

"Look, so I had an idea."

"Yes?" She said, still bending to the daisies. She wasn't trying to be rude to him, especially after all he'd done and the time he'd spent, but there was something glinting in the early light beneath tender green stems. It caught her eye.

"It's been a hell of a year, Beth. We both could use some time away."

She bent a little closer. Just beneath the mulch was something metal. She reached her hand out to it.

"Hey, don't let your coffee get cold, now," he said, standing and picking it up for her. "We should get away for a while, huh? Just you and me; we can get out to the coast, see the beach."

She wouldn't listen to him now, her hand reaching through the flowers to the glinted object. The daisies pulled towards her trembling hand, drawn as if by static.

"Okay, come away from there now."

"Wait, I see something."

He set her coffee down.

"I said come away from there."

"Wait a minute."

He crossed the path toward her. Beth was acting weird about the bed, as if she knew.

She stood and turned. Dirt clung to the cold steel of the revolver. She held it in the palm of her hand, her eyes wide.

"Christ, put that thing down," he said.

"A gun?" She asked. Then she turned back to the flowerbed, dropping to her knees. She set the gun beside her and clawed at the daisies, ripping their roots. Petals landed all around her as she dug beneath them with her bare hands. Dirt caught into her hair as she threw it behind her. She stopped; standing over her, Jim could see the same red cloth as her own coat, dirty and damp.

She gasped and recoiled in horror, falling back onto the path. She looked up at him.

"You," she said.

"No."

Beth gathered the dirty pistol to see if it would still fire.

Chaste

David C. Hayes

Spring thaw. Spring cleaning. Spring forward...or is it back? Regardless of which time zone Andrea Martin found herself in, the advent of spring always brought with it a sense, but only a sense, of foreboding. Maybe not even foreboding. Dreadful excitement, perhaps.

When speaking to the select few other humans that shared her worldview, Andrea would make the following analogy: spring and what comes with it, is like starting a new job that you are wholly and completely unqualified for; but it's the best paying and most fulfilling experience imaginable.

Andrea chuckled to herself as she made her way through the quiet little suburban neighborhood, shopping bag swinging at her side. Her neighbors waved as she walked by and she returned the greetings.

This spring would be even more important than the last few, but the people that shopped next to Andrea and took turns on the neighborhood watch, believed she was just like them. They didn't have the first clue. This spring Andrea turns twenty-seven years of age and she had been chosen for the most improtant task that her people could ever ask of her.

As Andrea walked and greeted, the shopping bag reassuredly tapped her leg in rythm with her footsteps. Although unmarried, much to her immediate neighbors chagrin, Andrea's bag was filled with infant formula and pacifiers. 'It's good to plan ahead,' Andrea was told, and she instictively rubbed her abdomen. Although a virgin, proudly and oddly so, considering her physical attractiveness and playful personality, Andrea knew that the groping hairy hands of men were not her destiny.

It was spring, the spring of her twenty-seventh birthday and on the Equinox the Dark Lord himself would rise from the bowels of his earthly prison and take Andrea's virginity.

Andrea smiled at the thought and actually looked forward to the pain and the tearing and the blood. For, after the Equinox, when the Morning Star retreated back into the Abyss, she would carry his child to term. And who would her neighbors wave to then?

Andrea continued to smile as she passed, not hinting in the slightest that it was nearly all over.

In Full Bloom

Kurt Fawver

The first buds appeared in central Pennsylvania not long after the last snow cover had melted. Within weeks, similar buds were reported in every state and every nation in the northern hemisphere. Thick, royal blue, vine-like and veiny, they were like nothing any botanist had ever seen. Beside all the other infant crops and flowers of the field, the tentacular vines were goliaths; by early April, their circumferences rivaled those of weightlifters' forearms. The strange plants were informally dubbed "slugweed" and, although the only resemblance to their namesake was in their cylindrical rotundity, the moniker stuck.

Initially, no one really tried to hack away at them. Lawn mowers and weed whackers seemed somehow too pedestrian to remove these uncanny, alien invaders. Even farmers delayed their planting season to marvel at the sheer strangeness of the vines infesting their lands. So, for a few weeks, the slugweed was only a target of camera lenses and prosaic news reports.

As spring rains began to buffet the land, however, the novelty of the vines grew stale. Crops needed space, parks needed beautification, and yards needed manicures in order to maintain their social standing. Civilization demanded that the slugweed become a subject to the blades of human will and progress.

But it refused.

Cutting the vines only increased their size and tensile strength. If mowers chopped them to the ground in the late afternoon, they regrew, twice as long and twice as thick, by the next morning. Digging them out was an impossibility, too. Slugweed root structure was organized like a vast Escherian circulatory system shooting infinitely into every dimension of space. Not even the most persistent backhoes could completely scoop them from the ground.

The world of chemical solutions was equally impotent, as no known herbicide inhibited slugweed growth or regeneration. Acids, bases, even fire and freezing: all had no permanent effect. The vines might singe, might shatter, might even briefly dissolve as if by ancient magic, but in twenty-four hours, they would be back, indomitable worms stiffly reemerging from the earth.

By the beginning of May, slugweed had overrun every pasture and dell north of the equator. Any patch of arable land, no matter how minuscule, was choked by royal blue vines. Diversity within the vegetable kingdom disappeared; famine was on the tip of the global tongue.

Third world nations began to starve in more earnest. Tiny envoys bearing international aid were dispatched to these impoverished countries but only as hollow gestures of solidarity. Mass food-producing first and second world nations knew that they had to conserve nutrients for their own peoples and livestock. After all, slugweed was entirely inedible. Consuming its vines or its roots led to vomiting, diarrhea, internal bleeding, and, in some cases, death.

And still, it continued to grow.

Trees, bushes, and grasses that were in close proximity to slugweed wilted, crackled, and died. Ecosystems changed to dictatorships overnight. Animals disappeared. Scientists made a dire pronouncement: the amount of oxygen in the atmosphere could be halved if the vines continued to expand their influence over the photosynthetic realm. All life but for the slugweed, which seemed to gain its energy from unknown processes, might cease to exist.

Populations began to move southward, running from the fecund apocalypse in a mass exodus to autumnal places. Vines began to encase homes and businesses, churches and libraries; they strangled every monument to human ingenuity. The great cities of North America, Europe, and Asia were swallowed under sapphire jungles. Half the world was abandoned to slugweed.

Months passed and millions of people—those too impoverished, too infirm, or too stubborn to become expatriates or refugees—passed with them. Breathing became a conscious chore. Still, there was hope. The southern hemisphere was intact and its spring was only weeks away. Delicious chlorophyll-laced buds would soon appear. Life would, seemingly, persevere. Smiles even crept back onto some gaunt faces.

And yet, for all the smiles and optimism, every eye remained fixed to the soil, knowing but not knowing that somewhere in a fallow field in Argentina or Australia, South Africa or Suriname, the seeds of death were already planted and soon, much too soon, their indigo sprouts would bloom in full havoc.

SUMMER

Erin Beiber's Wild Ride

Douglas J. Lane

It was old, battered. Jimmy surmised it had been assembled and disassembled a thousand times before stopping in the Jamesway parking lot.

"No way," he told Peter. "It's a deathtrap."

As if to punctuate the point, the six-car train rattled past them on a downhill, stirring the humid air. The roller coaster drowned out the cacophony of the midway—the barkers and music from the carnival's other rides—that filled the Saturday night.

"Wuss," Peter declared, and the pack of boys with him—a pack Peter didn't run with— followed his lead.

"Baby."

"Ginny."

"He'd probably cry like a girl."

Joey shrugged. "I heard three kids were killed last year over in Pinesville when the Flying Bobs came loose."

"I heard you piss your bed," Peter said, and threw an unwelcome arm around Erin Beiber. Erin had been standing beside the line talking to them, blue eyes and braces framed by her summer-bleached hair. Her sun dress announced her victory in the race to puberty. Peter had already allowed a couple groups to pass in line so he could continue talking to Erin, alternating glances between her eyes and her budding curves.

Erin shoved him hard in the chest and walked away. Jimmy saw a look in Peter's eyes that spoke anger.

"Bitch," he muttered. "C'mon. Ginny can stay here with the other girls."

The pack laughed as they formed up their line at the roller coaster—the Python, according to the sign in front with a dozen bulbs burned out.

Jimmy heard Erin behind him. "They've made a terrible mistake."

Jimmy turned and saw her staring at the ride, her eyes glassy. The air around them became thicker. Jimmy thought if he touched her, they'd arc electricity.

"What do you mean?"

"Sometimes I see things in my dreams. On Monday I saw him," she pointed to the guy running the Python, a thirty-something carny in a Phish t-shirt, "when they were setting up. His wife called and asked him for a divorce. He got distracted."

Peter and the others whooped as they boarded the coaster. The carny pressed a button. The chain caught the bottom of the string of cars and began dragging it up the first hill. Erin continued through the clanking. She might have been narrating a film strip.

"The bolts at the bottom of the first drop are too tight. On the next run, the torque from the train will finally sheer them off. The track will separate. The cars will jump the rails and crash into the framework. Ricky, Barry and John will break some bones. Tony will lose his left arm. Kevin will be crushed. Peter will be decapitated by the beam."

The cars crested the hill, rounded a curve, pitched forward into the first drop. Jimmy watched them plummet, man-sized bullets. He heard the shouts of excitement.

A metallic grunt punched through it all. Jimmy turned away as the first car sailed from the track. The screams of excitement were silenced by the shriek of twisting steel and an unnatural thunder, replaced by different cries of terror.

People rushed past Jimmy and Erin. He watched her staring at the carnage he couldn't face. A siren rose in the distance.

"You said you saw this on Monday," Jimmy said, his heart a kettle drum beneath his ribs. "Why didn't you tell anyone?"

Erin exhaled. She'd been holding her breath. "One night last month, I saw Peter when he was sixteen. He and two other boys forced me to do things. Horrible things. With them." She turned her cold gaze on Jimmy, and he understood what she meant. "Who would have believed me? This is better. Don't you see?"

She began to walk away through the swirling throng of onlookers stretching for a glimpse of the Python. Jimmy's stomach churned. He shivered through his sweat. "What about me, Erin? Have you ever dreamt about me?"

She turned back. Her expression was weighted with an unfathomable pity, a beguiling absence of joy. Then she was swallowed up by the chaos of the crowd.

Kite

R. Gatwood

The brat's death is declared an accidental hanging. Too bad she had to snap a branch off his maple as she went—but that's all over now, and, for the first time in weeks, the vision of that flailing, purple-faced thing outside the window weighs lightly on his mind. He opens the curtains; uncovers the pool, takes a beer out to the float; breathes.

It's a perfect August day. The sky is clear. Above him a red diamond circles, dipping lower and lower. It has no string.

Lobsters of the Damned

Lorna D. Keach

Jay's grandpa used to say: *You know the four seasons in Kansas? Too hot, too cold, too windy, and too much Road Construction*—and that was the joke that went through his head as Jay went head-first through his windshield on I-70.

A road lobster got him. His grandpa also used to say invisible road lobsters hunkered down on the steaming-hot road tar in work zones and waited to hitch a ride. They'd clamp down on an oncoming car's tires with their claws. Sometimes they did just fine, rode with their host to wherever they needed to go, flinging around and completely imperceptible. But, sometimes, they clamped too hard. The bits of rubber from blown-out tires strewn about the shoulder, baking in the sun—that was a road lobster at work.

And Jay thought about road lobsters as his windshield shattered, slicing up his face and snapping the vertebrae in his neck. As jagged glass lodged in his teeth and throat, he wondered just what he'd done to piss them off.

But, the road lobsters were a neutral force, his grandpa would've said. They just wanted to go somewhere, and their little legs kept getting trapped in the tar.

So they preyed on the innocent and hoped for the best.

Jay's pulverized skull hit the wet concrete and rebar in the old right lane, the lane they blocked off to finish this summer. The lane that had been blocked off all summer, every summer, because the 'Season of Road Construction' was eternal in this state. Jay drove through the interstate work zones every weekend to pick up kids, but this weekend they'd miss him. His blood splattered out into the gray muck, as thick as the tar that seeped into his wounds. Screaming metal and singing tires screeched somewhere in the distance, but Jay barely noticed because of the glass in his ears and the cement truck barreling towards him.

He couldn't move. But he could see. He blinked, too far gone to feel pain, and he saw them.

Cluttered around the orange cones, they sat, clicking their

claws and staring at Jay. Hundreds of them, twitching their eyeball stalks, their carapaces blackened and warped and spiny, like nothing Jay had ever seen in a tank. Their claws were deadly sharp. Their eye stalks looked on with cold, alien intelligence.

But Jay knew them. As the cement and the hot road tar seeped into his soul, blackening him, trapping him, one of the lobsters of the damned scuttled up to the edge of the concrete and clicked. For a second, something flashed in that one's eyestalks, something old and familiar that liked to tell bad jokes about the weather, and Jay thought about his grandpa, who'd died in a wreck on the interstate in 1992.

He thought about his grandpa as the black tar wrapped around his soul like carapace.

I'm on my way, Jay clicked at his lobster grandpa. Of course, as the cement truck rumbled over and pulverized what was left of his corpse, Jay knew he'd never really get anywhere ever again.

Bringing Home the Beach

Rebecca L. Brown

The shadows crept back a little, the short, brittle days lengthening into golden ages. She pushed the jumpers to the back of her cupboards, pulling forward the beach towels to take their place, shaking out the lingering remnants of last year's sand.

The last time she had visited the beach, they had been together. She remembered holding his hand as they walked towards the ocean. They had rented a little boat and taken it out, bobbing up and down on the increasingly choppy waves until they had been forced to go back to shore.

He had always loved it there, would head out to the beach even when it was raining if she'd let him. It had been endearing at first, then increasingly frustrating. Every night, the sand and salt caught between his toes had seeped out of his sandals across the floor; she had given up sweeping. The little shells and stones he collected for her had mounted up until she ran out of places to put them.

It was almost as if he wanted to bring the beach home to her, she thought.

Over time, he had become distant from her, more and more a creature of the waves until she had accused him of having an affair with the ocean itself. Once, when she had kissed him on his sunburnt cheek, she had been able to taste the salt in his stubble, the ocean's own salty kiss. All the money he wasted on silly things like boats and ice creams when she was saving for their future; he told her she had changed. She slapped him across the face.

That night, she had gathered her things and left him.

The little piles of sand on the floor were deeper than she had expected; these towels needed a good wash. She had thought they were already clean but sand was trickling off them in a steady flow. She frowned. The flow had quickened again, the piles becoming miniature dunes, sand seeping between her sandaled toes. She stepped backwards, kicking a cloud of sand into the air. Gritty, glassy little grains flurried in through her mouth, prickling her eyes until she fell. The towel, still gushing sand, landed on top of her. Somewhere in the distance, the seagulls laughed.

Summer Solstice

Chad McKee

His face was no longer just red, but actually peeling off. Blood was oozing out now, but there was no smoke. And it was taking much longer than it did in the movies.

Billy was still satisfied. He nodded to Barry and Paul sagely. "You see, I told you the light would do it. We didn't even need that other stuff!"

Barry crept up a little closer, shielding his eyes from the sun. It was a blazing day, not a cloud in the sky. He carefully kept the creature in the light, fearful that he might have some residual power. Billy's foot kept it down though. It was still muttering something. It sounded like 'skin friction.'

"What's it saying?"

"The same thing over and over," said Billy. "Just nonsense."

"Or some evil spell," put in Paul, keeping well back. He was scared when they originally came upon it, bundled up in a shawl, cap, and coat. The figure underneath was small but its outfit was frightening. All black, the color of demons and monsters. Who wears that on such a sunny, hot day? He and Barry would have stayed clear if not emboldened by Billy's swift action. Billy was also the fastest, always the leader. And he was a big boy for twelve.

"God," said Barry thickly. "It's horrible! Do you think there's more?"

"I don't know," said Bill. "But I bet it came from up north."

"Like the North Pole?" asked Paul.

"No, fool! North of town. Mama tells me there's some place for weirdoes up the highway."

Paul shivered in spite of the heat and Barry backed off the writhing body. More of these? Maybe they should make crosses and raid the Winn-Dixie for garlic after all. Paul voiced his concerns.

"No way. These guys are no match for that," Billy pointed to the fiery ball in the sky. There was no sign of cloud coverage any time soon and it was only after lunch.

"You see that bloodsucker?" he asked the Melting Man. "We've got, oh, another seven hours of that, I'd say. It's the summer solstice, you evil freak."

"What is the summer solstice?" asked Paul.

"The start of summer, dummy." He leaned in closer to the vampire, putting more weight on the foot, crushing its windpipe. "The longest day of the year."

Billy felt good. He was saving the town from this evil interloper—how could he not? He was Van Helsing, casting Dracula into the light of good.

The thing was struggling to get its hand from its pocket. Billy wasn't going to let it, but didn't want to unpin his foot, either. A gloved hand thrust itself out. There was enough space between glove and coat to see a small sliver of very pale skin. Like its face, the flesh turned red instantly and its weird, spider-like veins popped out in shocking contrast.

"It's got a tag on its wrist," said Barry.

"What's it say?" asked Paul.

"Barry, get up here and read it."

Barry made a face of extreme reluctance that was no match for Billy's stare. He knelt in close, not wanting to touch the thing for fear of infection. Could vampirism be passed merely by touch? He pushed the glasses up on his nose and squinted, cursing his nearsightedness.

"Well?"

"Exum pig-man-tos-um."

"What?"

Barry repeated the strange language but it was obviously something foreign— Transylvanian? Wasn't that where these monsters came from?

"There's a number and it says Berg Hospital."

This information was perplexing to the boys. Too much to do much but stare at the burning creature.

"Skindition!" it cried. "Skindition!"

"Something with skin," said Barry, who had a funny feeling in his stomach. Why would a vampire be at a hospital? Maybe it was being treated. "Um, I think I'm going home."

"Me, too," said Paul, looking green

"What? It's not dead!"

Billy watched as the two smaller boys picked up their bikes

and made for home, both giving nervous glances back. Sissies.

"Well, we're not going anywhere are we?"

The monster cried and repeated its esoteric chant. Its eyes were clouding. Billy figured it was dying. He almost took his foot off but sudden fear stopped him. He was alone now. Maybe it was pretending. Maybe it was waiting for Billy to take his foot away and then pounce on him, fangs bared. They hadn't noticed any fangs, but there could be, couldn't there? Best to wait it out. Billy was beginning to regret how early it was in the day; he was pouring with sweat, the perspiration running into his eyes.

The vampire was squinting fiercely but there was no longer fear in its eyes. Only hate. Both of its hands were out of it pockets. Billy looked around for sticks or rocks the thing might hit him with. None in sight, but underneath his body? He didn't know. He wiped sweat off his brow with his shirt and looked at his watch, then the vampire. It still stared at him maliciously. Billy thought it would have to die before he lifted his foot. But there was still six hours of sunlight to go.

Nature is a Cruel Beast

Robert Essig

Thick, humid air wafted into the house like sauna steam. From the porch came the sounds of nature's most crude, inapt musical instrument, every grinding stroke like fingernails on a chalkboard.

Things had been different sometime ago. Roy remembered the summers of yore, and though the humidity remained constant and unchanging, everything else had become permuted in one way or the other.

When Roy was young, he always enjoyed a midnight dip in the pool during the trying days of summer, crickets chirping their wondrous music, fireflies dancing in the air like stray embers from an unseen fire. He would collect fireflies in a jar and sometimes rub their phosphorescence on his face and chest so he too would glow in the night.

Sitting on the couch, waiting for his life to finally run out, Roy couldn't believe he had once actually wanted to glow like the fireflies. Now, that seemed preposterous.

Oh, how his ears ached from Sue's constant cacophonic grinding from the porch. She used to pick a banjo—several years ago before the change—and now that she was unable to pick up a musical instrument, she did her best with what she had, only she didn't seem to get any better night after ear-bleeding night.

Nature could be a cruel beast.

The silence haunted Roy's heart. With all the windows open in the house, there should have been a symphony of crickets and the miscellaneous hoot of an owl, only now there was a low moaning hum that seemed to carry nicely with the wind, and Roy loathed it. It sounded like agony, wholly lacking the beauty nature once achieved.

Then there were the bugs that used to crawl into the house as if to seek refuge from the heat, dying and leaving their carcasses in the corners and along the walls. They were a staple of summertime in Arkansas, the spiders and mosquito hawks and moths and other such winged insects that seemed to fly into the house as if it symbolized, to them, a great mausoleum.

Even that had changed. Roy sat there on the couch when the first crawler of the night caught his eye, making its way along the baseboard like spiders and bugs used to do unnoticed. Now, he couldn't help but notice, and it was the very reason he would have to turn the lights out and pray Sue would give up her futile attempt at recreating the music she once loved.

The little crawler stopped, exhausted from the long haul into the house, some kind of preternatural instinct driving it forth, or perhaps an ancient memory embedded in its miniature skull. It looked up at Roy, and he knew right then that the lights had to go out before any more wandered in, because he couldn't take their empty, forsaken eyes.

Roy wanted to say, 'I'm sorry,' but he could neither speak nor apologize for nature's wrong doing. The little man who wandered in, his moaning call of misery singular to the constant moan of his brothers and sisters outside, far too much for Roy to take on this summer night.

He turned off the light, and on his way back to the couch through the dark room he heard a tiny yelp as he stepped on something, and had he been capable of tears, he would have shed one for the unfortunate that had been in his clumsy path.

But even the dark hardly saved his tortured mind from the realities of nature's flipside, for his abdomen was always aglow on nights such as this one, casting an eerie phosphorescent brilliance that could never remind him of those fond memories as a child collecting fireflies in a jar.

Sue finally stopped sawing her legs. God help him, Roy could now close his eyes and hope that he never wakes up.

Swarm

George Wilhite

We were scouring the area, running counterinsurgency along the DMZ of the Reorganized Eastern States, surely the worst post imaginable for a grunt in the last civil war during the summer. Nearly a hundred degrees and ninety-eight percent humidity. We walked stealthily through the thick Appalachian Forest looking for traitors and deserters.

That day had been routine, killing those on the known terrorist list on sight and interrogating the others, usually ultimately killing them too. Taking prisoners was too heavy a liability. The country was overcrowded, even after five years of war, so there was no place left to build any kind of prison.

And much of the day and all through the night, we battled my most hated enemy of all, the fucking bugs. I have an irrational, but intense aversion to insects, and a special hatred for mosquitoes. Fate was providing plenty of payback for all the times I killed the pests on site, whether or not they were actually doing me any harm. Some days, there seemed to be so many of them I thought we would be sucked dry.

It was around dusk when the events of that day turned from mundane to remarkable. Suddenly we heard some damn fools shouting for our attention. Responding quickly, mostly to just get them to shut the fuck up before they blew our cover, our platoon found three drafted civilian scientists huddled around a corpse, busily checking out readings on their field equipment.

Sergeant Corelli snapped at the civvies. "What in the name of Mother Mary are you clowns sounding off about?" Before they could answer, he continued his barking. "You dumb asses are gonna get us killed. The cowards are everywhere and some of them are armed, you know."

While Sarge continued his abuse, I saw their faces.

Remember, these are white coats I'm talking about. They'd certainly seen plenty of disgusting shit in their laboratories, all their guinea pigs, human and otherwise, dying in horrific ways as the Reorgs looked for an effective biological means of combat, knowing all the while the rebels were doing the same thing on their side of the border.

And still, these white coats looked scared—no, more than that—*petrified.* This corpse rotting on the ground must have been more than just some rebel piece of meat.

Finally, one of them managed to get a word in between Sarge's tirades. "Listen, sir, you need to hear us out, and quickly, or it won't matter who's our friend or enemy or who's hiding from who. We're all in deep shit already if what we suspect is true."

While he was speaking, all three of them had put on their masks and without waiting for orders from Sarge, we grunts did the same.

Adjusting the airflow on my tank and breathing normally again, I looked at the body that had the civvies' panties in a bunch. No gunshot wounds or any other signs of combat injury. The only blood visible was seeping from his eyes, nose, and in a puddle flowing from the seat of his pants. But the real horror was the poor bastard's flesh. The best way to describe it was to say it looked doughy. Flabby, like it was barely hanging onto the bones.

"We found this body twenty minutes ago," the civvie continued. "Most of the deterioration you are seeing has transpired since then."

"What are you saying?" asked Sarge.

"We think the enemy exposed this subject to their newest agent of destruction and then just dumped it off here."

"To expose us," one of the others added.

"Airborne?"

"We put on our masks as a precaution but the tests we just ran seem to suggest blood borne."

"So what's the issue? He isn't going to be infecting anyone now as long as we steer clear of him. Get that flame-thrower over here and burn him." Sarge ordered.

"It's not that simple," the civvie doing most of the talking stated gravely. He pointed to the sky. "When we found him, he was covered in those."

The sky was darkened by a preternaturally large swarm of mosquitoes. The enemy must have seeded those God forsaken woods with the ravenous insects before leaving the host of their new virus behind.

Darkness fell as the swarm descended, fed, and then moved on, indifferent to their significance in a bloody human conflict over petty differences.

The Sands of Cangrejo Azul

Dan Larnerd

The view from the dunes was breathtaking. A crystal blue summer sky seemed to melt away into the warm waters around Cangrejo Azul. Dipping into the waters were mile after mile of luscious deserted beaches crowned with lazy palm trees.

Gary didn't notice that though. As he carried a white and red cooler down the beach trail, his eyes were locked on a different vista—the two local girls he had met the night before.

Hypnotized by their skimpy bikinis, Gary lost his grip on one of the cooler's handles. He stumbled forward and caught the cooler with his knee before it tumbled into the sand. The two girls turned and giggled together. Gary grinned sheepishly at them as he hefted the cooler back up.

"Are you okay, Gary?" Paloma asked.

Smiling, Chelo said, "It's not much further."

"Don't worry 'bout me..." Gary blushed. "I'm... ummm... solid."

The girls giggled and continued to head down to the beach. Gary took a deep breath and started after them.

"I'm solid?" Gary muttered to himself. "Could I sound stupider?"

The girls raced down onto the sand. They began to spin and dance as they laughed. Gary breathlessly watched them take off their bikini tops and run into the ocean.

"Now's your chance, Gary! Don't blow this!" he said to himself.

"Come join us!" Paloma shouted as Chelo tried to tickle her.

As fast as he could, Gary bounded down to the beach. He dropped the cooler onto the sand and ran out to the two young women in the surf. They shouted with glee and began to splash water at him. He splashed water back, making them squeal in delight.

A little bit later Gary was sitting in the warm sand. The two girls were sunning themselves on both sides of him. As Gary dug a cold beer from the cooler, he stole glimpses of their bare skin.

Chelo caught Gary looking her over and smiled. He turned away and blushed.

"Chelo and I are really glad you came, Gary. This beach is a really special place for us," Paloma said.

"I'm glad I… uh… came, too," Gary stammered.

Chelo took the beer bottle from his hand. She smiled at him and put the beer bottle's neck up to her full lips. With her smoky eyes fixed on him, she took a slow drink.

Gary swallowed hard and squeaked out, "When you asked me to meet you, I was afraid you weren't going to show."

"Why would you think that?" Chelo asked.

Gently, Paloma put a hand on Gary's shoulder. She moved in close to him and just before her lips touched his face she softly pushed him backward until he was lying on the sand.

"I've never had much luck with American girls. And you are both so pretty…" Gary said.

Seductively, Paloma held out a handful of sand and poured it down his chest. He couldn't help but nervously gulp as Chelo reached across him to pick up a handful of sand and let her breasts dangle in his face.

"Paloma and I just know how special you are," Chelo said as she poured her handful of sand on Gary.

"This is so great," Gary grinned as they continued to pour sand on him.

As the girls continued to bury him, Gary said, "You guys wouldn't believe this crazy old man. He saw me talking to you. He said—"

"What did he say?" Chelo asked, and dumped a big handful over his chest.

"Forget about it," Gary fumbled.

Paloma laughed, "Tell us what the old man said."

"Seriously, I shouldn't have said anything."

"Now you have to tell us!" Chelo said.

Paloma laughed, poured some more sand on Gary and added, "Yes, tell us!"

Gary fidgeted under the sand.

"Like I said… I shouldn't have said anything."

"Just tell us!" Chelo said, faking a big frown.

"He was talking so fast. He said if I went with you I would get… crabs."

Gary shook his head as all hope of scoring vanished.

"At least that's what I think he said. He was talking so fast and my Spanish isn't too good. Maybe he really said something else."

Both girls laughed and after a moment Gary joined in. They continued to pour more and more sand over his body. Soon Gary was buried in sand up to his neck.

The two girls stood up and picked up the cooler. Gary went to sit up and discovered he couldn't move. He couldn't even twist his head to see the girls walk away.

"Hey, what's going on?" he screamed.

"We've got to go!" Chelo shouted.

Paloma yelled, "Her children will soon be here!"

Struggling in the sand, Gary hollered, "Whose children?"

A small blue crab popped out of the surf. It was unlike anything Gary had ever seen. The impossibly smooth shell was like polished turquoise shimmering in the summer sun.

It was joined by another crab and then another. They scuttled toward Gary as he screamed. Soon a flood of blue crabs filled the beach and swarmed over him. He struggled in vain as their small claws began peeling the flesh from his screaming skull.

Precious Youth

D. G. Sutter

Beth sat on her wrap-around porch in a white rocking chair. The fresh paint smell hung on the roof sheathing, which jutted off the Victorian house and over her head. The chair rolled forth and back in liquid motion and her curly red head rested against the wooden boards.

As she relaxed, Ty plucked the remainder of the weeds along the foot of the shed. When done, he sauntered up the steps and stood with the Louisiana heat glistening off his black skin. His shadow covered Beth's eyes.

"All set, Ms. Harper," he said.

Elizabeth motioned to the small table where a twenty dollar bill and a pitcher of lemonade sat. Ty crumpled the bill into a ball and jammed it into his jean pocket.

"Care for a glass of lemonade?" Beth asked the young man.

Ty removed his baseball cap and wiped his forehead with the back of his hand. "Shore would, Ms. Harper."

The prepared glass filled with yellow drink. Ty put the rim to his lips and swallowed half.

"Have any plans fo' the summer?"

"Me n' a coupla' friends thinkin' bout driving down to Florida." Ty finished his glass and placed it hard on the table.

"Sounds like fun. I only been once, myself."

"That's too bad. It's a lovely state," Ty said.

Beth thought of how little she had traveled. She had planned to do more of it, but never quite had the money. "Better carry on home, now. Before yo' Momma starts to worry boutcha'," she said.

Ty bid Beth goodbye and jogged down the road, grabbed his bike from against the beech tree and rode off. Beth envied his youthful energy, his ability to move with such ease; the carelessness of his composure. She stayed on the porch until the sun started to set. Ty was long since gone when the sky changed from magenta to plum.

Through the tunnel of trees walked a man in a fine white suit, supported by a cane and engulfed by the brimmed hat on his head, which matched his clothing. When he reached the bottom of the stoop, he looked up with a kindly face covered in white stubble.

"Good evening, Ma'am," he said.

"Can I help you with sumthing?"

The old man grinned, "Well, I sure hope so. It was a long walk down. I'd like to buy this here property."

Beth chuckled. "I didn't see no for sale sign in the front yard! This house ain't for sale. It's been in ma' family for five generations. Before the Civil War, ya see?"

"If I proposed I could make you young again?"

The old man dropped his cane into the dirt and bent one leg on the bottom step and stared into her eyes.

***

Ty pedaled down the dirt road. He was due to mow the grass for Ms. Harper, but it was a hot one and he wasn't particularly looking forward to it. The house was adorned with an old man on the front porch, instead of the chubby woman. The man drank lemonade from the same cup Ty had used two days before.

"What can I do you for?" the old man asked Ty.

"Is Ms. Harper in?"

The older gentleman shook his head dismally. "Why no she isn't. Ms. Harper don't live here no more. She done gone and sold her soul to the devil."

Upstairs a young girl sat in a white rocking chair. She stared out the window at the exchange, her curly locks bouncing as she rocked and played with her dolly.

Beneath the Pond

G. Elmer Munson

Sheila stomped through the woods, puddles splashing her flip-flops and raining mud on her toes. She knew the area well; she'd spent half her life walking aimlessly and enjoying the voice of the woods. Sometimes the trees would talk to her and tell her things that were going to happen. Her family thought she was crazy. That suited her fine.

She ran as fast as she could through the moisture that remained after the summer's rain. Nothing spoke; instead, something followed her. Although all she could see were glimpses of things moving quickly out of her field of vision, she could hear them tramping through the brush, crushing twigs and breaking branches along the way.

Sheila looked towards a patch of brush where the ground sloped downward. *Maybe a place to hide*, she thought. She moved down the slope, holding onto branches for balance. Loose wet earth slipped under her feet as she ran. Ahead, she could hear water. It wasn't the light trickle of flowing water; somehow the stagnant lull of a murky pond beckoned her.

She spotted the glimmer of water between the branches and set off towards it. The things were moving close; she could feel the malevolence spreading through the trees. Once she reached the edge of the brush, she grabbed handfuls of branches, ripped them aside and plunged headfirst into the thick.

Thorns scratched her face and cut her legs. Blood mixed with sweat as she raced for shelter. Her feet sank deeper with each step. Other noises mixed in with the lull of the pond. Things moved in the brush; they crawled through the trees joining with the things following her towards the water.

To her left she could see one of them. A dark blur scrambled through the branches on its way towards the pond. She couldn't tell what it was; though it moved like an animal on all fours, she could see no arms or legs.

There were others moving along side of her. She moved faster, not worried about the blood she spilled along the way. She was close to the edge, she could clearly see the water waiting stagnant under the windless sky. Behind her, twigs snapped and branches broke. She turned and saw one of the things heading right for her.

Because of the path she had already cleared, it followed faster along her trail. She turned back towards the pond, frantically clawing her way forward. She could feel the rage pouring off it like steam from an overworked engine.

Sheila grabbed at branches and screamed her way through. Thorns ripped chunks of hair and flesh as she broke into the clearing. She slipped in the mud and fell backwards into the pond. She gasped for fresh air, wiped leeches from her face, and spit out the putrid scum from the surface.

The beast came up to the water's edge and began circling the perimeter. Sheila scrambled backwards towards the center. Soon others joined. They moved so fast they blurred together as they ran. She sat in the water and screamed until something grabbed at her body from under the pond's surface. It snagged her hand and pulled it down into the muck.

She tried to scramble backwards but it had too firm a grip. The things surrounding the pond began to howl as they raced. About a foot down, her hand stopped at a hard object. She grasped what felt like a shoebox and pulled it up. As soon as it broke the surface, the things stopped running. They seemed to bow, slithering away from the water.

She held up a rotting wooden cask, the clasp dangling rusted and useless. She opened the lid to reveal a leather book covered in wet earth. The things backed into the woods, leaving Sheila alone.

"You saved me," she whispered.

"Not saved," a voice in her head replied, "acquired. We've got plans." She stared at the dark leather for a moment before pulling herself up out of the muck. As she walked, she could see the things on the outskirts of her vision escorting her home.

They were guiding me, she thought, *not following*. Her cuts and scrapes faded; her muscles no longer ached. She felt better than she had in years. She held the book up and looked at it in the sun. It felt warm, seeming to vibrate in her hand as it glowed.

"I think you and I are gonna get along just fine," she whispered. "Just fine."

Chant

Carl Alves

Adam Vaughn loosened his tie as sweat beaded on his forehead. The steamy August afternoon was making his skin crawl. He hated driving to the central sales office located in this concrete jungle. Whenever he drove there, he fretted about someone breaking into his car. The city people were nothing short of animals wearing clothes.

The sales meeting had been pointless. They always came out with these new-fangled sales techniques and computer systems they forced you to use. He had been selling medical supplies for twenty-five years and could sell circles around these newbies. It was a waste of his time.

The car had better be where I parked it. That was all he needed today.

A loud noise came from the block ahead. Adam's brow furrowed. Probably some stupid protest. Those idiots were always complaining about something. He hoped they had not blocked off the street where he parked since he still had two sales calls this afternoon.

As he got closer, he couldn't make out what they were shouting. *Probably some ethnic thing*, he thought. *What a bunch of losers.*

He crossed the street and the noise got louder. It sounded like a riot. Part of him wanted to leave right away. He didn't need this crap today. But the part of him that wanted to find out what was happening forced him to slow down. If there was a shouting match or a fight, he had to see it.

They were chanting. "What the hell?" *What was it some religious ceremony*? *A loony, fanatical group*? The city was full of them. Loonies, thugs, and thieves, you couldn't get enough around here.

He reached the end of the block. The noise was coming from an adjacent alley. His car was in the other direction and he had to leave soon, but it wouldn't hurt to take a look.

"Eight, eight, eight…" They repeated the number over and

over again.

Why in the world would they be chanting eight? He looked at his watch. It would eat at him all day if he didn't find out.

Half way down the block, the chanting grew louder. Across the street was a large, jagged cement wall from a partly torn down building. The chanting was coming from behind the wall, but it was too high for him to look over.

Adam scanned the wall and found a peephole sized opening in the concrete big enough for an eye to peer through. This way he could find out why these people were chanting the number eight. He stooped over and leaned his face in. He then closed his left eye and looked with his right.

Blinding pain shot across his face. He screamed in agony, not sure what happened. The pain was unreal. He backed off and everything was blurry. He could only see with one eye. He blindly groped the air, still screaming and felt his right eye protruding from its socket, a knife stuck into the cornea. He ripped the knife out and staggered away, howling at the top of his lungs. Behind him the chanting started. "Nine, nine, nine, nine…"

Soup Bone

Matt Kurtz

Mamma left him in the car again while she shopped. It made very little difference that the windows were cracked an inch when the sweltering temperature outside read well into the triple digits. Had she even taken into account that his entire body was covered with thick fur?

Apparently not. Mamma was only thinking about the money she'd save after reading the store's circular ad earlier that morning over breakfast. In the kitchen. Back at the house. The cool, air conditioned house.

With tongue panting, he peered through the heavily tinted pane of glass that separated him from the world, watching as the people entered and left the store. There was still no sign of Mamma. She had said that she'd only be a few minutes. That was over an hour ago. So where was she?

His wagging tail fell still.

It was getting way too hot inside the vehicle and who knew how much longer Mamma would be. Although he was told to be a good boy and stay quiet, he thought about crying out to be noticed. He felt forgotten. Abandoned. But drawing attention to himself could prove disastrous. The authorities would be called in and he'd be taken away from Mamma.

But maybe she needed such a scare. She'd definitely think twice about leaving him unattended in the hot car again. Maybe she needed to be taught a lesson.

He'd show her.

His head raised and back arched, ready to sound out a guttural howl. The store's automatic doors slid open and Mamma stepped out. He paused and looked closer at her. She was pushing a fully loaded shopping cart across the sizzling asphalt and wincing from the bright sun.

Poor baby. Was she uncomfortable?

Mamma loaded the trunk with all her bags of bargains. The automatic locks popped up, causing the ears on top of his head to do the same. She opened the door and gasped when the heat rose out of the car, blasting her face. “My word!”

Waiting on the backseat with his head hung low and eyes pitifully staring up, he heard her slam the door, start the engine, and crank the air conditioner to full blast.

After wiping the sweat from her brow, she turned around, finally acknowledging him. “Oh, I’m so sorry, baby!” she said, leaning over the seat. “Mamma took a little longer than expected.” She went to give him a good scratch behind one of his ears.

He pulled back.

“Oh, baby. Don’t be mad at Mamma.”

He slid across the seat, moving away from her.

She sighed. “I know it’s hot. And I’m sorry. Tell ya what. How about you sleep in Mamma’s bed tonight instead of your cage? Would ya like that?”

He looked away. Not good enough.

“Okay, okay. Ya know Mamma’s making soup for dinner, don’t ya?”

His eyes shifted back to her. His tail twitched.

“That’s right. How about you get the soup bone after I’m done with it?”

He licked his chops, his pink tongue running over his canines. His tail sprung back to life.

“So I take it that I’m forgiven?”

After a slight pause, he nodded. “I guess so.”

She smiled. “That’s what I like to hear. Now let’s get you strapped back into your car seat like a good little boy.”

As they drove home, he thought about his time spent in the scorching automobile. It really hadn’t been *that* bad. For tolerating only an hour of pain, he’d be the one getting the coveted soup bone tonight, something that was usually reserved for Roscoe…the family dog.

Lost in a Good Book

Adrian Ludens

Maggie looked up from her book and realized the girls were gone. She scanned the empty beach and threw a panicky look toward her sedan. She saw no one.

They were here a moment ago. Maggie glanced at her book and flushed. She'd been so absorbed in it that she'd lost track of time.

If the girls had gotten bored… Maggie spun in the direction of the surf. She broke into an awkward jog. The sun glared down at her snidely. The sand grasped at her feet and slowed her progress to the universal speed of nightmares. The surf hurled itself toward her spouting indecipherable insults and then retreated with derisive laughter.

"Lindy! Lila!" she screamed. Only the gulls cried in mocking response.

They'll charge me with criminal negligence. Something bobbed in the surf twenty yards out. Maggie lost sight of it behind a cresting wave. She splashed in deeper and broke into a doggy paddle. Her arthritis wouldn't let her do more.

"Lindy!" Maggie called again. She choked on a mouthful of saltwater and began to flail. She'd gone further out than she had intended and felt disoriented. Maggie paddled on doggedly. "Lila!" Sorrow overwhelmed her. She'd lost her darling grandbabies. *If they find us all later, at least they'll know I tried. I tried...*

Maggie held onto this thought as she sank and the undertow swept her away.

***

The girls returned to where Maggie had left her book and looked around, perplexed.

"Where's Grandma?" Lila wondered.

"I dunno." Lindy responded. "I told her we had to go use the potty."

Lindy and Lila sat together in the sand and played as the sun descended. At last it sank completely into the water and it too was swept away. Later, when it started getting colder, the sisters crawled into the back seat of Grandma's sedan and wait for her to return.

Repellent

Melissa L. Webb

John walked into the kitchen and set the package of paper plates on the counter. He glanced over at his wife, who was busy preparing a large salad. "Are we almost ready?" John asked as he slipped his arms around her.

Kelly looked up at him. "Yeah, we just have to barbecue the steaks. Everything else is ready."

John smiled. "Our house-warming deck party will be perfect, thanks to you."

"You give me far too much credit, John," Kelly said, kissing him lightly. "But I'll take it."

John laughed as he walked over to the fridge. "I bet you will." He pulled out a few six packs and started to put them in a cooler. "Oh, that reminds me. Did you get the repellent?"

Kelly looked over at him. "Yes, I got the repellent. This is me we're talking about."

He looked at her. "You sure? I don't want any of our guests bitten tonight. That's all people talk about. 'I went over to so and so's house and ended up with bites all over me.'"

Kelly sighed. "Will you relax? Everything will be perfect. I've lit those special candles and torches and placed them all over the backyard. Those nasty creatures won't set foot near our party."

John frowned as he rearranged the bottles in the ice. "I sure hope so. Those bites are painful. I hate those blood suckers."

Kelly walked over to him. "Here," she said, handing him a spray bottle. "I even got some to spray all over us. There won't be any biting tonight. I promise."

John lifted up the ice chest and headed for the backyard. "I just hope the stuff really works."

Kelly followed behind him, carrying the bowl of salad. "It's already working, John. See for yourself."

They stepped out through the sliding glass door and onto the wooden deck.

John squinted out past the flickering flames into the darkness edging around their backyard.

Rows of hungry looking monsters stood around, held back by the fumes put out by the burning repellent. Their fangs glistened in the light as their glowing red eyes locked on to the couple on the deck.

"See, I told you," Kelly said and laughed. "You worry too much. There will be no biting tonight. This vampire repellent works like a charm."

Summer Night

Rubilec Mendoza

First summer. Lucy knew it could be the last day. Still, she had not felt the heat of the sun. She'd longed for it for her eight years of living. She envied the other children who played under the sun without getting rashes or blisters on their body. She wished she had the skin of a normal person.

Lucy slept with tears on her face. She was hugging her giant teddy bear that was the same size as her. It was also as white as her.

She'd been right. The afternoon of the next day welcomed the first drizzle. Just a few more days and she'd see her tutor again.

Day one. Day two. Three. One day to meeting math and science and English. The heavy rain abated on the afternoon of day three. Maybe it would return this evening.

Lucy went out to see the foggy world. She was wearing a thick jacket with a hood that almost covered her entire face. She wanted to play so she'd asked permission from her mother who was busy at the kitchen. She had promised to just stay outside and not go far from the lawn. But she broke her promise. She followed the wet road outside their house. Seldom did cars pass through this road in their suburban community. She walked fast without pausing. There were just a few residences in their neighborhood. The haze was becoming thicker as she went further. She stopped when she saw a girl of her age playing jump rope on the road side. Lucy talked to the girl, and in a moment they were playing together. The girl's name was Alice. She said they came from the city and her family was here because it's her grandmother's birthday.

Lucy and Alice became instant friends. Lucy said she had to go because her mother might be looking for her. She went away smiling. She walked and walked again but because of the thick mist she lost her way. She took a muddy trail which she thought would lead her home. It was a path nobody took anymore.

The rain came.

"Mommy!" Lucy whimpered. She turned and she ran while hugging herself. The trail was muddier now. Lucy thought she'd heard someone laugh. She felt even more afraid. She did not notice the protruding rocks on her way. Her left foot got caught in between them and she stumbled. Her head hit a rock hidden in the mud.

The rain blew harder and in that hidden untraveled path Lucy had taken, the soil was eroding, covering her little body in mud.

***

Second summer. Alice thought of the girl she had met the last year when they'd visited her grandmother for her birthday. Alice was in this quiet place again. She wished she could stay here longer this summer.

Alice lay on the bed with a smile on her face. She prayed she'd see Lucy tomorrow. She would ask help from her father to find where Lucy lived.

The air was warm so Alice slept without her blanket. She hugged her white teddy bear because its fur felt cool to her skin.

Alice was sweating when she woke up. She left her teddy bear and turned the light on. She stared at her watch and after recalling what 7 meant, she figured out the time was 10:35.

With small steps, Alice went downstairs to the living room. Her parents, grandmother, and Uncle Jim were there. Her mother who was standing by the door saw her.

"There you are Alice. I was about to go to your room. Come here, honey."

Alice felt something was going on. She could tell it from the look of the faces of the adults. She pretended to sleep on the sofa and listened to their conversation. Then, she learned that three people had been found dead in the neighborhood just tonight. They had been seen with a knife in one hand and their own skin in the other hand. They had apparently sliced off a portion of their skin from a part of their body.

Alice's parents decided that all of them, including Alice's grandmother and Jim, would go to the city the next day and no one would come back to this place until the mystery of the deaths was answered.

Jim stayed in the living room to watch over his niece while Alice's parents and grandmother packed their clothes.

"Ugh. It's so hot," Jim murmured to himself and swore many times under his breath. Alice heard it all and she thought her uncle shouldn't curse the weather. He shouldn't curse at all. It's bad.

Alice slept for a while. Then, she woke up thirsty. She got up and went to the kitchen. Her uncle Jim was in there. Alice hid near the door because she saw her uncle with a knife in his hand. She screamed when she realized that Jim was trying to slice off the skin covering his left thigh.

Morning came. The mighty sun appeared. Alice led her father to the place she dreamed about last night after she'd witnessed her uncle hurt himself. Jim was brought to the hospital but Alice and her father stayed because she pleaded for it.

Now they were in the spot. Alice's father recognized the place as the trail they used to take when he was a child. It was not being used anymore.

Alice knelt to the ground and she drew the grass that had grown on the dry soil. They saw a petrified face that had surfaced on the ground. Alice knew it was Lucy. The summer heat had dried and shrunk the mud that had covered her. Her face emerged but nobody saw her. Nobody listened to her calls, only Alice.

Speed Demon

Ben McElroy

Exceeding the posted speed limit as usual, Martin's Mustang approached the infamous Mill Street Curve. He sped up and took the hairpin turn rather sharply. As a result, his car almost rear-ended a slow-moving Chevy Malibu.

"That jackass is only doin' twenty," he said to his girlfriend, Darla.

Martin honked his horn. The other driver ignored the taunt. Just as The Curve began, Martin started to pass the sluggish vehicle.

"I don't think you should do that right here," Darla said.

"Just shut up and let me drive the way I want," he said.

When his Mustang was next to the Malibu, Martin honked again and flipped off the other driver, who reduced the Chevy's speed. However, after Martin passed the Malibu, it never drove more than two car lengths behind the Mustang. It even followed Martin and Darla into the Leicester Drive-in.

During the opening credits of the first movie, *Sleepaway Camp*, both vehicles pulled into adjacent spots in the front row. Martin glanced over at the Malibu.

"That loser in the Chevy won't leave us alone."

"Let's move. I don't wanna deal with any of that road rage bullshit," Darla said.

"This douche bag's gonna get his ass kicked," Martin said as he got out of the Mustang.

The Malibu's driver, a very tall and skinny man, also exited his vehicle and said, "You have to slow it down on Mill Street. A lot of people have lost their lives on The Curve."

"I drive how I want," Martin said.

Walking over to the lanky guy, Martin threw a punch at the dude's face. But the man suddenly changed and now looked all mangled and rotten.

"What the fuck?" Martin asked in a strained voice.

Grabbing Martin by the shoulders, the dead thing said, "The Speed Demon won't let my spirit rest. It'll do the same to you unless you heed my warning and start driving with more caution and respect!"

Martin tried to escape the animated corpse's grasp. He only managed to pull decayed flesh from its forearms. Roaring in frustration, it shook Martin.

Then it said, "Why won't you listen to me? The Speed Demon intends to claim you. Tonight."

As soon as the words were uttered, Martin's attacker and its car vanished. He ran back to the Mustang.

After starting the engine, he tore out of the drive-in. Martin and Darla drove in silence. Through the open windows, a humid breeze caressed their heads.

Turning onto Mill Street, they saw the dead man's Malibu blocking both lanes. Martin slammed on the brakes and shifted into park. He quickly locked his door with a trembling hand. Darla remained quiet, though she shivered fiercely.

Martin scanned the road for the rotten guy. He saw him up by The Curve standing in front of something. Anger overtaking his fear, Martin exited the Mustang and rushed over to confront his adversary.

Before Martin could utter a word, the other man said, "Do you see this white cross behind me? That's where I died ten years ago because I couldn't care less about the rules of the road. And the Speed Demon stole my soul. Sometimes, though, I escape from the Realm Between The Shadows to help people like you. But *It* always finds me and brings me back."

Martin gazed at the cross. Then he went over to it and kicked it a few times until it fell over.

The dead man and his Malibu disappeared. The nefarious Speed Demon took their place. It grabbed Martin, carried him to the Mustang and tossed him onto the roof.

As the grotesque beast slid into the driver's seat, Darla screamed. The car roared to life. The Speed Demon raced over the asphalt. Martin did his best to cling to the roof. Nearing The Curve, The Speed Demon cackled as the speedometer reached eighty.

The wind's constant pressure soon flung Martin into the air. Spinning and flipping, he saw the Speed Demon wave to him.

As Martin fell to the ground, the Mustang veered into a telephone pole and burst into flame. Then pain erupted throughout his entire body as he landed on his back and skidded several yards before smashing headfirst into a tree.

***

After recovering from a fourteen month coma, Martin was eventually able to operate a vehicle again.

He continued to drive with reckless abandon.

Vanity

Michael Clifton

Gerard woke as the sun began its stretches, limbering up for another assault upon the city. He unstuck himself from his mattress and made his way into the kitchen. "Showers still not fixed. Useless country!"

Sarah ignored him "We leave in five minutes, hurry up."

He sulked back to his room and stripped down, boxers clinging like a second skin.

Gerard, posed in the mirror trying to find something to admire, loathed the figure he saw. Abs, which had taken a year to sculpt, were now encased by a shield of pasta induced fat; once lean biceps, transformed into jelly-like lumps. He wanted to smash the mirror and the pig it contained. He looked just liked '*them*' he thought, thinking of his family. He tried styling his hair with gel, but it collapsed, resting on his scalp like a lizard.

It was the weather; the heat wave had struck Europe the week after they had arrived, suffocating everything. Naturally, his ever frugal sister had rented the cheapest possible apartments for their trip. Air conditioning was out. Dodgy areas and broken plumbing was in. Ten minutes later, with Sarah glaring, they departed.

Summer in Europe had brought images of wonderful nights, and gorgeous girls. Instead, it delivered rundown apartments and days of sightseeing, surrounded by hordes of poorly dressed sunburnt tourists. His sister was the worst, priding herself on her coupon clipping fashion sense.

As they drove through the streets of Florence, he cursed his father for allowing her to handle the money. "You're just mad because you got rejected again. She must have been what, nineteen? Better off going for girls your own age. You're not the twenty-five year old stud you once were."

"At least someone in our family takes pride in their appearance. If you were less tight with cash, I could eat healthy and I wouldn't be turning into this," he said, grabbing his stomach, feeling revolted at its touch. He wanted out, to be back in New York, at his gym. He would need to lose weight before returning. To waddle in like this would see him turned from a king to court jester. The thought unnerved him.

They arrived to find a lengthy line of tourists waiting to see Michelangelo's David. By the time they reached the ticket booth, Gerard had endured an hour of prattle about Italy's beauty. A burst sewage pipe could thrill these people if it happened in Tuscany, he thought. He hated being surrounded by these package holiday tourists. Sarah was right at home, but for Gerard, who pictured himself a class above, the wait increased his frustration about the day, the city, the whole trip.

A woman jostled him from behind, He glared back . "Sorry," she lied. Back home a hick like that would know her place, he thought. After spending years, and a good chunk of money sculpting his body, three months backpacking had reduced him to just another chubby American standing in line, a second rate chump. To hell with David, "I'm off." He didn't wait for a response from Sarah.

Outside the heat had conquered all. His unwashed gel laden hair, turned into a pool of grease. Oil-like drips stained his best shirt.

Walking into a café for water, he saw the waitress who had rejected him last night, seated next to a young man; interlocked hands indicating it wasn't her brother. He sat behind them attempting to get a glance at his rival's face, who, to Gerard's chagrin, spoke with an American accent. He wanted to compare himself, to see if he measured up. His rival was in his early twenties well built; handsome with Elysian hair.

The boy noticed Gerard staring at them, Gerard was sure he saw a smirk, little brat. Back home, Gerard would have had that girl by now, single or not. It wasn't his fault he had been forced to survive on pasta and pizza, that he hadn't been able to shower. This wasn't who he was. He heard a laugh and knew someone was laughing about him, the fat, greasy loner in the corner. He fled outside; the sun savaged him as he walked aimlessly.

He wandered into Piazza della Signoria, where flocks of tourists were getting their photo taken in front of David's replica. He wanted to cut that face; it was a mocking swipe at the frailties and weakness of the human race. It stood there never aging, flawless, while Gerard was growing old, stuck in his stinking body, trapped in clothes too tight. He rushed up and spat at its feet. Someone yelled. Gerard replied with his fists; this trash couldn't judge him, he was once as glorious as this statue and he was real! Hands grabbed him, Gerard struck with his bottle, glass gouged flesh. He didn't hear the policemen's warning, but he felt their shots; Gerard slumped to the ground, screaming obscenities. He felt blood and began losing consciousness.

The final image he saw, the one that would sever Gerard from reality, was David's face. High up, not a drop of sweat visible, untouched by the heat, taunting Gerard with a smile only he could see and whispering the words, "You're just like the rest of them."

Summer Break

Tony Nola

Albert's favorite time of the year was summer break. He enjoyed working outside in his straw hat as the sun beat down upon him. Every summer, at exactly 11 a.m. on a Sunday, he would mow his lawn like clockwork, just one of his many traditions for this time of year. The long days of pleasant sunshine made him appreciate the life he had.

Albert cleaned off his old workbench with turpentine to get rid of all the nasty stains that had been imprinted since the last summer. Next, he swept the small remnants of dust into the trash. He prepared his tools for the summer; his hedge clippers were carefully and slowly sharpened to cleanly cut. His gardening gloves were washed by hands in his sink with bleach. All the items were placed carefully, but snuggly, into his little green bag. He was ready to go.

He walked two blocks and sat in anticipation for the afternoon bell, the last strike for three months. The ten gallon garbage bag was large enough for the pests that would be by soon. The tools were sharpened and the workbench ready. A small smile stretched across his face as he waited in anticipation for the summer festivities to begin.

FALL

I Change the Leaves

Scott Cole

It's my time of year. Finally. This summer was a long one. The heat, so oppressive. I'm happy to see it go.

Most people love the summer. They have their barbecues, and their empty weekend getaways, and their drunken, naked beach parties. But not me. I stay tucked away, all summer long, hidden in my house. And I wait.

But things are changing now. It's my time of year. I change the leaves.

There's a certain kind of crispness in the air now. You can smell it even. It's the best time of year for a stroll around town. Some days I just walk and walk and walk.

I love the feel of the old buildings here too. I run my fingertips along them as I pass. I press my palms against their stone foundations. They're cool, just like the air is turning.

The wind is soft. It's constant, but calm. It calms me.

I see the trees reflected in the windows downtown. They're waving at me, welcoming me into my time of year, and I smile.

I change the leaves.

I see the people too, rippling along the windowpanes. They're sad about the season. You can see it in their faces. Smiles turning downward. Their tanned skin already beginning to fade. They don't understand.

I reach up. The branches tic against each other, and make tiny sounds as they scrape along my wrists, my arms. I grab a leaf. It's harder and smoother than I expect, its edges uneven. I wave it around in the air, so happy.

Because it's my time of year.

The people see what I'm up to, and they approach. But they don't understand. They look at me with frowning faces, but the more they frown, the more I smile.

I want to show them all how wonderful my time of year is. How perfect.

I take my leaf and dip it in the nearest man. But he yells at me—doesn't like what I'm doing. I pull it back, and it's a bright, beautiful, gorgeous red.

Leaves are meant to change and fall, so I lay it on the ground.

I grab another from above, and dip it in an old woman. She doesn't like it either, so I take it back and set it down. She starts to cry.

I take another, and dip this one in a child's ear. I love the way the color changes. So vibrant, so pretty. He falls asleep.

This is my time of year, and the leaves are turning red. I take another, and I dip it.

I take another and another and another.

I change the leaves.

Blue Ribbon

Dan Larnerd

Behind the dusty old tarp, something let out a fierce grunt that caused everyone in the county fair pavilion to turn.

"Hush, now," Old Man Olsen whispered.

Old Man Olsen stood in his old wool coat with his snow white hair under a black sea cap. With his hands shoveled deep in his coat pockets, he looked like a poster child for curmudgeons. Along with all the wrinkles on his face, he wore the grim resolve of a man on a mission.

"I'm surprised to see you here, Mr. Olsen. I thought you'd be packing," Maxwell Chase said.

Olsen sneered at Chase who was standing on the muddy hay-strewn floor in three-hundred dollar Italian loafers and a thousand dollar suit.

"Every fall for the last forty years, a pig from my family's farm has won the blue ribbon at the county fair," Olsen spat.

Chase laughed, "Going out with a bang?"

He slapped Olsen on the back and laughed again. "I think it's cute. Here you are. A man who is about to lose all he owns and you're still trying to impress a town that could care less about you."

"I'm not here to impress them," Olsen snapped.

"Good!" Chase said. "After a petition without signatures, being shouted down at Town Hall and even Reverend Bluth suggesting you be committed… You now realize you don't impress anyone."

"Why don't you just leave me be, Mister Chase?" Olsen scowled.

"Because I had to wait all through the spring and summer before I could start work on my housing development. Now the very last piece of red tape has been cut," Chase hissed. "This town has spoken! Next week your shit smelling pig farm gets bulldozed. "

Another loud grunt came from behind the tarp.

"No more fighting this thing!" Chase said, wagging his finger at the old man. "As they give you that last blue ribbon, just remember this: These people want Olsen Farms out and Chase Estates in!"

With that, Chase put on a big smile and walked into the crowd. He shook hands with Reverend Bluth and the Mayor. They all stood in a tight circle and chattered. Laughing, they stole glances at Olsen.

Old Man Olsen stood defiantly by his stall until the judging started. The Mayor and the rest of the judges went down the row of stalls. Olsen's pig was at the very end.

"I do love showmanship!" The Mayor said. "Show us what you got behind the tarp, Mister Olsen."

"Sure," Old Man Olsen muttered.

The crowd gasped, as Old Man Olsen ripped down the tarp. One of the lady judges stumbled backward with the back of her hand pressed against her forehead. Mothers shot up and pulled their frightened children from the pavilion.

Inside Old Man Olsen's stall was a monster. It was a pig the size of six pigs. Rippling muscle upon more muscle stretched under its thick leathery hide. Two tusks the size of scythes jutted from its broad snout and a coarse Mohawk-like mane spiked down its head and back.

It snarled and smashed its head into the steel bars of the stall. They bent back as it pounded into them again and again. The giant pig let out a squeal that was pure demonic rage, making the audience jump.

"It's an abomination unto the Lord!" Revered Bluth cried out.

Old Man Olsen shook his head and said, "Naw. I just took the seed of last year's prize hog and inseminated the biggest boar an Alabama game preserve had ever bred. Couple of thousand dollars in growth hormones and steroids, you know like the ballplayers use, and there you all go."

The Mayor gasped, "It's hideous!"

"I call him Junior." Old Man Olsen smiled.

With that, he sprang open Junior's cage. The giant beast thundered out of the stall and plowed through the judges. The mayor went soaring across the pavilion and collapsed into a bloody heap.

Terror seized the audience. Junior smashed through rows of wooden chairs, plowing through the members of the city council. Reverend Bluth was gored across the midsection. Spectators leaped out of the way and ran for the exits. Shattered bodies went sailing through the air as half a ton of angry pig bowled its way through the mob.

Maxwell Chase scrambled toward one of the exits as Junior's focus turned toward him. Running for his life, Chase knocked down the town's senior librarian and elbowed his way for the door. He screamed as the giant pig charged. With one vicious thrust, Junior impaled him on both razor sharp tusks.

Old Man Olsen laughed manically as his creation lifted Chase into the air and roared victoriously.

That's when Old Man Olsen noticed something at his feet. Floating in a puddle of blood was this year's blue ribbon.

As panic and carnage spread out before him, Old Man Olsen calmly picked the blue ribbon off the ground and wiped it clean on his coat. He held it high over his head and laughed as Junior continued to rampage through the terrified crowd.

Beneath the Trees

Lawrence Conquest

June's hand felt small in Ballard's own, like a child's. He clutched her tighter to him, thrilling at her touch. So young, so precious. And tonight was the night. Tonight he would reveal his true feelings for her. Tonight he would reveal his love.

"Is it much further?" she asked, looking up at him with wide blue eyes.

"No. Not long now, and then we'll be ready."

The trees above seemed to sigh in response, a melancholy echo of their burgeoning love.

"Are you sure you don't mind?" asked June. "Telling everyone, I mean." She didn't like to talk about the secret nature of their relationship, didn't like to remind Ballard of the age difference between them. She knew how much it upset him.

Ballard swept an arm before him, encompassing the forest. "First we'll tell the trees, and then we'll tell everyone else. I'm tired of keeping this a secret, June. You know how I feel about you."

June lowered her head bashfully and smiled to herself. She still couldn't believe that this had happened to her. That someone like Ballard could come along and just sweep her off her feet. She couldn't wait to tell her parents. Oh, she knew Ballard's age might cause them concern at first, but when they saw how he treated her, how romantic he was, she knew they'd be convinced. The fact that he wanted to carve their names in the forest spoke volumes of his romantic nature. Some of these trees must be hundreds of years old. To think that their names would endure through the decades. She hoped their love would last forever.

"This'll do." Ballard had stopped before one particularly large oak, its autumn foliage rustling in the gentle breeze like an extravagant crinoline petticoat. A pale moon peeked shyly through its upper branches, dappling the ground below in a cool azure light. A single russet leaf dropped from the tree, arcing down in a series of gentle waves before coming to rest among its roots.

"I'll start then, shall I?" Ballard removed a utility knife from his jacket and began to carve his name into the bark. "First me, then you."

June cast her gaze about her as Ballard worked, wondering if any other couples had been this way.

And then she saw it: regular lines carved into the bark of the maple opposite. She moved closer. The wounds were ancient and partially scabbed over by sap, but still legible. Two names, surrounded by a carved heart. The first name was EMMA. The second was BALLARD.

"What?" June felt light-headed. Short of breath. She backed away from the tree, as though it was malignant. Alive.

"You're not my first, you know." Ballard had stopped carving, and looked at her with concern.

June tried to tell herself not to be silly. Of course there'd been others. Ballard wasn't a young man, he must have had lovers before. Long ago.

And yet when he reached for her, she flinched and backed away. Turning, June steadied herself against another, maple, its leaves a buttery yellow in the evening light. Her fingers traced out the letters of the names carved in its bark. BECKY. BALLARD.

June threw herself away from him, plotting a random path through the forest, heedless of the branches that snagged and hindered her. And on every tree she passed she saw a carved heart, and within every heart she saw two names. SAMANTHA, BALLARD. LAURA, BALLARD. SARAH, BALLARD. JACQUI, BALLARD.

June's vision began to blur as the tears clouded her eyes. She tripped, fell—and was caught. Strong hands gripped her by the shoulders and pushed her towards the nearest tree.

"Why?" she gasped. All she could see before her was bark, its surface scored with ancient veins. The man held his body tight against her. Close, like a lover.

Ballard leaned over and whispered in her ear. "Like the trees, everything has its season. But you'll never grow old, June. This way, you'll always be young. For me."

June felt the knife being pressed into her grip, Ballard's hand encircling her own. Knife in hand, she was powerless to resist.

"First we carve the tree—and then you."

Ballard pushed her hand down and the blade began to cut. Sap welled like blood, sticky and dark.

Something creaked above her and June looked up. A wind had sprung up from nowhere, whipping the branches above into a violent melee.

"What the hell?" Ballard winced. Something had stung him. Rain—no, not rain—leaves. Ballard reached a hand up to his face and it came away wet with blood.

And suddenly the air was full of leaves, the pregnant trees shedding their spawn en masse as though responding to some silent signal. But where the contact should have left papery kisses, instead they struck Ballard like shards of glass, cutting through his clothing and slicing the flesh beneath.

Ballard held his hands above his face, screaming aloud as they were lacerated by more falling leaves. Desperately, he looked for June, but the girl was moving away from him. She seemed to be running down a corridor of calm, the deadly leaves falling on everything except her.

Ballard thought he could hear voices, and tried to tell himself it was just the wind through the trees. A root ensnared his foot and he dropped to the floor. He could feel his body bleeding from numerous puncture wounds. He pulled the tattered shreds of his shirt away from him, intending to fashion protection for his face, but stopped short at what he saw.

The cuts had not been random. The leaves had scored names into his flesh. Those who had gone before. So many girls. So much pain. So much anger.

Turning on his back Ballard looked to the sky for forgiveness, but the falling leaves took his sight away from him, by and by.

One Night Stand

Angela Alsaleem

Todd's head pounded as he tried to open his eyes. Sunlight glared through dappled shade and he shut them again. He tried to remember where he was, but the effort made his head ache more. He tried to sit up and couldn't.

The bar. He'd been at a bar last night. Had he driven drunk? A car accident may have thrown him. He squinted. Stalks of corn towered around him, their golden leaves rustling in the breeze. He couldn't move.

Head too muddled, he tried to yell, but pain seared his lips.

"No, don't do that. You'll tear the stitches," a woman said. She crouched over him and gave his mouth a slap.

The slap brought him back to himself. Memory glimmered. The woman from the bar. She'd asked if she could take him home with her.

She squatted behind him and with a grunt, heaved him upward. His stiff body moved like a board. His head reeled in the ascent. His body jolted and he stopped moving. She did something at his feet, muttering to herself then she stood and tugged at his clothes. He was bound to something that felt like a splintery post. It scraped his back and poked at the back of his head. His eyelids fluttered as he gasped. The world blurred into focus. A field of corn tassels swayed at eye level.

The reek of rotting meat wafted around him. Confused, he relaxed his neck, allowing his head to loll as he examined himself. He wore a plaid shirt and tattered jeans, both stained and stinking. These weren't his clothes. The deep brown stains unnerved him as well. Too much like blood.

She adjusted something on his head causing bits of straw to fall over his eyes.

"You're perfect," she said. His stomach clenched and his balls tightened.

His throat felt parched, mouth dry, filled with something pokey and sweet. After exploring with his tongue as best as he could, he thought it might be more straw. Pain pierced his lips as he tried to scream.

"I said don't do that." She glared up at him, the trace of a smile in the corners of her eyes.

His heart pounded. He jerked in his bindings. She did something behind his back and the rope pulled tighter, digging into his arms. His fingers tingled then went numb.

She chuckled. "You're all the same, you know? You'll go home with anyone so long as you think you'll get your dicky sticky." Her syrupy voice, that had enticed him back at the bar, now dripped with venom.

"You stupid bitch," he tried to yell. Nothing more than muffled shouts came out.

She laughed and ran a knife across his forehead. "That's so they can smell you," she said.

Blood ran into his eyes. He gagged, but managed to swallow the bile before it filled his mouth or came out his nose.

"I'm not an object," she said and petted his face, smearing the blood. "None of us are." She walked away.

He cried, unable to stop himself.

"Wait," he tried to scream. "I'm sorry." He knew she couldn't hear him, but continued to scream apologies and curses in equal measure long after she left.

Clenching his teeth, he struggled against his bindings and strained to look around him. Nothing but corn in all directions, as far as he could see.

And scarecrows.

One stood close enough for him to see that rather than a stuffed burlap sack for a head, the scarecrow had a rotting face. Straw protruded from holes in the cheeks.

A crow landed on his shoulder and cawed, the shrill sound digging into his mind. He swung his head at the bird in an attempt to scare it away, but the black devourer made a low squawking sound like laughter. It pecked at his earring. He screamed and shook his head. The crow fluttered back.

Todd looked at it, panting through his nose, the smell of putrefied flesh emanating from his clothes. Its head shot forward as it pecked first one eye and then the next, blinding him before he had a chance to react, the pain red and flaring. Hot goo ran down his face. He screamed and thrashed against his bindings.

Several more crows landed on him. Their harsh caws became his world as they fought over his eyes and the shiny earring. His flesh tore as they pinched and pecked and ripped. Their dusty feathers fanned the putrid air around him.

When the hole in his cheek gaped large enough for him to suck in deeper breaths, he felt a moment of gratitude. One of the crows pulled out some of the straw filling his mouth, and the cool air rushed into his lungs. It felt great until the same bird tore at his tongue.

As night descended, the crows left him to the bugs. He shivered as dew settled on his skin.

His last thought was of the large bug that crawled into his throat. He gasped in shock and it became lodged there, squirming as he choked. His body worked to breathe as his face reddened, the veins of his still intact flesh pulsating. But despite the pain, he felt relief. It would be over soon, and he would be just another scarecrow in her field.

Freshmen

K. G. McAbee

"I don't know, I just don't know." Jordan looked at himself in the cloudy mirror and shook his head. "I mean, why us? Why us, of all the freshman class this year?"

"Maybe these women have taste. Did you ever think of that?" His roommate Nick was trying to decide which of his two cleanest t-shirts was least objectionable. He shrugged and chose the red one. Red for lust, he thought. Hey, it might work.

"Yeah, right." Jordan pulled on his jeans. One knee peeked out of a rip. "We are without a doubt the bottom of the barrel. No, the scrapings from the bottom. No, the dregs of the scrapings from the—"

Nick held up his hand. "I get it, okay? We're not exactly in the top ten percent."

"Are you kidding me? We're not even in the top ninety-nine percent."

Nick shook his head. Jordan had issues; he'd known that from day one. But old Jordie was a good roommate. They hadn't met until the first day, but the computer had made a good match: both orphans, both going deeply into lifelong debt with student loans, both somewhere towards the lower end of the attractiveness scale. Still, it was cool having someone who understood stuff like that sleeping in a bed three feet away. Too bad Jordan snored.

"Well, how do I look?"

Nick eyed him, head cocked to one side. "Like you're going to prison, or maybe a chem exam."

"There's a difference?" Jordan asked.

Nick laughed. "Let's go before the Omega Cubed girls come to their senses."

***

Omega Omega Omega House sat at the edge of the campus, an old building with a surrounding cloak of trees and shrubs. Light shone out in a band from all the first floor windows, but the upper three floors were dark.

"I don't know, Nick. It's awfully quiet for a party, don't you think?" Jordan eyed the twin stone lions that sat on either side of the steps leading up to the front porch. Each held something in its open mouth, but the stone was so worn he couldn't make out what it was. "Maybe we got the date wrong. Let's go."

"Oh, no." Nick pulled a paper out of his pocket. "See. Today's September twenty-third, and that's what it says on the invitation. 'You're invited to our special equinox bash on September 23rd!'"

"Maybe we're early?" Jordan asked hopefully as he tried to edge back towards their dorm.

"No way. Come on; I'd hold your hand for you, but you're just not my type." Nick climbed the steps and beat a salvo on the brass knocker.

The door creaked open with a noise like a scalded cat.

But there was no one inside.

"Nick, come on, this is weird."

Then Jordan saw he'd been mistaken. Someone was standing in the doorway, her hand extended, a big smile on her red, red mouth.

"You must be Nick and Jordan," she said, and Jordan felt a shiver down deep in his belly. "Our freshmen guests. Come on in, please!"

Jordan didn't quite see how it happened, but suddenly he was up the steps and in a brightly lit room, surrounded by a dozen or so of the most beautiful women he'd ever seen. They kept pressing drinks into his hand and hand-feeding him the most delicious little sandwiches. He munched and drank and laughed and was having the best time he could remember in his life—ever.

One particularly gorgeous girl, her eyes as green as grass, whispered in his ear: "Let's go down into the basement, want to?" Jordan's mouth was full so he just nodded. He felt his temperature rising and his heart was pounding in his ears.

The green-eyed girl took his hand and led him across the room to a tall door carved with what looked like chemical symbols. He looked around and saw that Nick was right behind them, a blonde with almost nothing on cuddled up to him.

The door opened and they all four started down a set of steep, narrow steps that twisted first left, then right, until they finally arrived in a dim, cavernous basement draped with cobwebs and smelling like cat piss. The floor was stone and there was a circular brass drain in the center.

"Uh, this isn't the most romantic spot I've ever seen," Jordan pointed out.

"Romantic?" said the girl with green eyes. She was smiling at him, and he noticed for the first time how white and sharp her teeth were. "What would we want with romantic? This place is perfect for dinner."

"Dinner?" Nick asked. "I'm kind of full, actually. I didn't know we were invited to dinner."

"Oh, yes," said the blonde. "You were. And we all just love us some nice, fresh men. Don't we, sisters?"

The shadows in the corners coalesced to solid shapes, and the shapes all had big red mouths and long white teeth….

Harvest

Nathaniel Lee

It was harvest time. Torvald hated harvest time. It was bad enough with the animals, but at least there were only a few of them. He'd put it off as long as he could.

He hauled himself up into the tractor seat and paused. He turned his head to check the blades. They were in place, sharp and polished. He'd spent all day yesterday preparing them. He wondered if he should check the hitch again, or the oil might need changing or… Torvald realized he was stalling. He grimaced as he turned the key. The tractor rumbled to life, vibrating beneath him in that awful, familiar way. He drove it to the north field. The exhaust coiled behind him like a noxious serpent.

As always, the field was full of song. The high and piping voices of the grains mingled with the basso harmonies of the gourds and tubers. The corn was first to spot him, being the tallest.

"Farmer Tor!" said the nearest stalk, and the cry spread down the field, interrupting the melody. "Farmer Tor! Farmer Tor!"

"Have you come to water us, Farmer Tor?" said a pea pod. "It's still so early!

Torvald shook his head. "Afraid not," he said. "Not today."

Nothin' but Grass

Rob Rosen

"Rake it up, boy," grunted Billy's father, tossing him outside. "I don't want to see nothin' but grass."

Billy landed hard on his rump, hands scraping against gravel, skin ripping as a grunt got pushed up from his lungs. He turned his head, left to right and then back again, taking in the sea of red and umber, of brown and mustard yellow, leaves in every stage of decomposition. "But, Pa," he whined. "There's plumb near a million of 'em."

His father cackled, smoldering cigarette thrown to the ground. "Guess you better get started then, boy," he spat, slamming the door behind him, causing the frame to rattle. Even more leaves fell to the earth. A drop in the bucket, really.

Billy sneered, watching them eddy, whirling in the breeze in a swirl of color, his bile rising, burning through his belly, black as tar. "Nothin' but grass is just what you're gonna get, Pa," he whispered. "Just like you done asked for."

He grabbed the rusted rake, its prongs bent this way and that, the handle cold and hard beneath his grasp. Again he stared at the brittle sea, eyes squinted, watery, a salty tear streaming down his cheek, hitting his tongue like a bullet. "Nothin' but grass." His teeth ground together as that old rake of his pushed on through.

One pile at a time, dozens, hundreds, thousands of leaves. Oak leaves, maple, birch and beech, sycamore and magnolia. Rounded, serrated, etched and grooved. Color on top of color, until Billy's eyes blurred with it all, his hands blistered and red, the pain excruciating. Then grass, at last, grass. Brown and yellow and dry.

Billy smiled, a wicked, knowing smile, hands throbbing as it all got raised up, until nothing but grass remained. "Just like you done asked for, old man." He walked to the back stoop. "Nothin' but grass," he grumbled, knocking on the door, jumping back when it swung open, a blast of cold air stinging his face.

"Well now," said his father, yanking on his whiskers, eyes scanning the length and breadth of the massive yard. "Not a leaf in sight, boy." He walked to the middle, Billy still standing on the stoop, bloodied hand playing with a dangling cord. "You done good, boy," he rasped, the smile turning sour in a heartbeat. "Now go and do the front."

"Nothin' but grass there, too, Pa?" Billy asked, sarcasm dripping like Spanish moss off an old oak limb.

"Don't get smart with me, boy," warned his father, bony hand raised, bony finger pointing, trembling.

"No, sir," he replied, a giggle spewing out, the cord yanked with a hard tug. "Wouldn't want me gettin' smart all of a sudden."

And from the canopy dropped what Billy had been raising, hour after hour, leaf after leaf, thousands and thousands of them.

"Plumb near a million of 'em," he whispered, watching them fall, feather light. Though not when piled together like that. No sir, no how.

In a kaleidoscope of hues they rained down, obliterating his father in an instant, only his hands poking out, flailing, clutching at the air, not even the shouts and screams escaping through. Until only the pile remained. Death on top of death.

"Enjoy your grass, Pa!" Billy shouted, his voice lifted up on the frigid air, echoing out in all directions before the boy disappeared back inside, the door slamming behind him, shaking the very last leaf off the roof. It landed atop the heap, crimson and orange, thickly veined, where it sat, the eventual crush of sleet and snow pounding it all into the frozen dead earth.

Awakening

Michael Clifton

"Mr Pearson?"

Martin Pearson opened his door to a man he knew solely from email correspondence. He felt awkward, as though they were a couple on a blind date rather than two tenured academics. "Yes, I am"

"Ah, good. I am Jakob Wiacek."

"Thank you for booking this hotel, I—" Martin was cut off mid sentence.

"Nonsense, a pleasure to share my passion for the old gods with a fellow searcher."

Martin gave a self-deprecating snort. "Well I haven't found much, not even enough for an article, let alone a book."

"You found him, didn't you?" Jakob said softly.

Martin was about to ask what the remark meant when the elderly man clapped his hands together grinning wildly.

"Talk later, now we enjoy ourselves."

***

Walking through Gliwice accompanied by gangs of surly young men, Martin understood his afternoon would not be spent discussing European folklore or viewing local antiquities. Instead they headed to that modern shrine of communal activity: the football stadium. Autumn heralded the start of the season across the continent. Martin grudgingly joined the procession, attempting to hide his dislike of the chosen activity from Jakob, who seemed in his element amongst the shaven heads and tattooed biceps.

Jakob seemed respected and well known. They were waved through the turnstiles without paying, emerging into an air laced with abuse and rival chants.

The opposing fans were cordoned off by security and the two groups traded barbs and occasional missiles smuggled through the gates.

"We're a new club, not very large in numbers. We're building something special here though," Jakob yelled over the cacophony.

It was standing room only and Martin prepared himself for a long afternoon on cement terraces, naked to the autumnal wind slashing down, a forewarning of the coming winter.

The opening whistle blew and the crowd erupted in the mass hysteria that always made Martin wary of attending matches; the crisscrossing between violence and support seemed much finer in Gliwice than back in England. He buried his head into his shoulders willing the clock to tick faster.

As the game progressed, the chanting and abuse rose in tempo and aggression. Two men jostled past Martin, a blade of silver winked up at him. Martin decided to leave. "I'm off, need some fresh air."

Jacob's hand slammed down upon his shoulder.

"Everything you want is here. Stay."

"It's ok, I can interview you back at the hotel."

Jakob leaned forward, pulling Martin close. "This is the interview."

Sweat broke upon Martin's face, claustrophobia engulfed him. He wanted out, away, to be done with this horrible environment. He tried moving but was hemmed in. He turned back to the game trying to calm himself, looking for his chance to escape.

The chanting now became rhythmic, the Gliwice fans no longer screamed out random insults as their voices merged. Harsh as the sound was, it calmed him and soon his pulse beat with the chant. His mind began first; then, he noticed his voice whispering the words, gradually getting louder, not caring that he spoke no Polish. Soon, he was screaming with all the energy he could muster and then, as he lost himself in the chanting, the stadium became quiet.

His vision blurred until finally all was still.

"He called and you came. You belong."

Jakob's voice was clear in the silence. The crowd came back into focus except the sight he now saw caused him to kneel in terrified awe.

It flew in and out amongst them all, feeding off their energy, changing into shapes and patterns, creating symbols that Martin did not understand but desperately wanted to. His mind struggled to absorb what he was witnessing and, if as in acknowledgment to his supplication, a figure emerged, towering above the stadium, one belonging to the dark recesses of the subconscious. A primordial being, whose blood flowed through the Gliwice fans, who, in turn, willingly gave their blood so it could live. A reciprocal arrangement first forged in times when Europe was still a forest and its civilization not yet an embryo, now renewed centuries later.

Then, the noise returned and the vision dissipated.

Unknown hands passed Martin an object. He looked down, finding a knife. Jakob smiled.

"Those who honor him need have no fear."

Martin looked at the opposing fans, feeling a twinge of sympathy. Their violence was cheap, infused with alcohol and life's frustrations. Nothing like the force he felt coursing through his being. The whistle blew, he pocketed the knife.

"This is what you have been searching for all these years," Jakob said. Martin felt calm, happy. He felt home.

All thoughts of sympathy fled. He turned, instinctively joining a group of men darting into the side streets to hunt their rivals and to give sacrifice to a god reborn.

Remember Us

Sean Logan

It was a cold, crisp morning. The sun was low in the east and climbing. A few dedicated joggers could be seen here and there, like asylum escapees, their breath clouding up before them. The Stars and Stripes lined the block in various forms: windsocks, banners and, of course, flags jutting from every other porch like spears on an ancient battlefield. Sue stepped on the porch, balancing her briefcase, purse and a travel mug of coffee, and caught sight of the flags lining her block. She glanced at her own rusty flag mount next to the door and sighed, "Jon, you forgot the flag! It's Veteran's Day."

Jon grumbled from somewhere in the house. Sue grimaced, shut the door and left for work. She drove into the sun, squinting as she pulled the visor into place, and completely missed the band of soldiers walking down the sidewalk.

They had come from the same place, wore the same flag on their shoulders, but were from different times. Transparent shadows, some wore the drab green long coats and flat metal helmets of World War I, others the pot helmets of World War II and still others the jungle camouflage of Vietnam. Across the street a squad of desert-fatigued Marines advanced in pairs, leapfrogging from yard to yard.

They approached a house with no flag. The squad leader crouched and held up a closed fist. The others stopped. The leader made several hand gestures and two soldiers wearing black sunglasses unlatched the front gate and ran low towards the house. They stopped at the door, throwing themselves hard against either side. One of the men knocked on the door.

A full minute later the door opened and a man in a robe peered out rubbing the sleep from his eyes. The soldier who'd knocked raised his pistol and shot the man in the side of the head. His body bounced off the doorjamb and fell backwards. The second soldier reached around the door and tossed a grenade inside. Both men sprinted from the porch as the entryway exploded. A group of World War I soldiers found the next house without colors. They kicked the door in and disappeared inside. Gunfire and screams echoed throughout suburbia.

***

Jon heard the knock on the door as he climbed down the attic ladder, red, white and blue flag of the United States of America in hand.

"Coming." Jon tried not to knock anything over with the flag pole on his way to the door. He opened it and found himself staring at two guys that should have been saving Private Ryan. He thought he could see the street behind them, through them, but that had to be the morning light. "Yes?"

The soldiers looked at Jon, then at the rolled-up flag in his hands, then at each other. One of them shrugged. His partner tipped his helmet to Jon slightly.

"Thanks for the support, sir; the boys on the front really appreciate it."

Yard Work

Stephen Hill

Stepping outside Saturday morning at nine, Paul Bruin surveyed the pool of discarded color stretching out across his back lawn.

Fall cleanup was a weekly necessity on a property huddled up against a forest, but Paul didn't mind. With raking leaves, the rules were wonderfully clear: no management issues to deal with, no conflicts to sidestep, and certainly no political hierarchy to navigate. It was just straightforward, honest-to-God work.

What made the effort even more enjoyable was that when it came to raking leaves, he was miles ahead of The Dick.

From the moment that Richard Clomper (a.k.a. Dick, a.k.a. The Dick) moved in next door, he embodied the type of person Paul was predisposed to want to punch in the face. Barely 30 and practicing corporate law, he drove the latest Beamer, golfed in California, and looked like he modeled for Harry Rosen. As a final kick in the slats, his wife Janice was drop dead gorgeous, and a sweetheart to boot.

So, while staying ahead with the leaf raking wasn't much, at least it was *something*.

Paul stretched under the eighth straight day of streaming sunshine. *Today*, he thought, *I'm going to make the work last*. Glancing next door, a contented smile slipped from his face.

The Dick was raking his lawn, and, judging by a wall of leaves piled high on the property's edge, had been for a while.

Keep it together, Paul thought, panicked. The Dick was moving slowly. There was still a chance to beat him.

But he had to move.

Grabbing the rake like a weapon, he plunged it into the first cluster of leaves squashed against the back steps, and hurled them across the yard. Working fast, he drove waves of them forward, slamming at splashes of color. Thoughts of gloves were dismissed, and the handle chafed his hands raw.

He chanced another look next door and Dick was gone. The leaves were abandoned and—looking absurdly vulnerable—so was his rake.

Paul doubled his efforts, revitalized. The twang of the rake's prongs and the swish of the leaves were the only sounds in the autumn air. Cramps stitched his middle-aged muscles, but he ignored them. Victory was in sight.

Through the sting of sweat, he saw The Dick returning in a slow shuffle, a large red plastic container clutched in one hand. A red plastic gas container. The shape was as familiar as anything in Paul's garage, something used to feed his lawnmower and weed whacker. But there was nothing to feed on Dick's lawn—just plenty to *burn*.

Paul's eyes jerked towards the forest—towers of dry lumber over rivers of parched leaves—lining the borders of a hundred neighboring homes. Swept by escalating winds, a blaze would be unstoppable.

Paul threw the rake down. "Dick!" he screamed.

Dick's head turned like a robot's. A huge toothy grin broke across his face, and he started to pour. Gas drenched the leaves and grass, slopping over his shirt and jeans.

Paul began to walk towards him. "Hey!"

Still smiling, Dick pulled a cigar from a shirt pocket.

Paul was now running. He heaved himself over the backyard's fence as Dick flipped a matchbook open. The stink of gasoline clogged the air, poisoning it. A match sparked, lighting the cigar.

Paul came to a stumbling halt, taking in new details.

Dick's hair was a tangled mess, his cheeks slathered with stubble, his clothes striped with grime. Welts crisscrossed his bare feet, and dirt stained his toes. The worst though, were his eyes—glazed stones nested in bruised hollows.

"Uh, Dick?" Paul said, his voice shaky.

With the match burned out against his fingers, Dick took the cigar from his mouth. Tendrils of smoke drifted lazily from his lips as if from his brain cooking in his skull.

"Dick?" Paul repeated.

Dick's head cocked like a dog's. "Yes?" It was as if he was trying to do an impression of himself—and was failing miserably. A lump of ash broke from his cigar, and flakes dusted the grass.

Paul flinched. "How about we go in the house?"

Dick's face flickered with recognition.

"Finish the cigar where it's warm," Paul continued. He walked backwards and Dick followed, his legs as stiff as the trees.

"You're doing great," said Paul. Speaking as if to a pet, he had a sudden, crazy urge to slap one knee. "Nice and easy."

"Easy," repeated Richard. His mouth twisted, as if he didn't recognize the word's taste.

"Good," Paul said, wondering where the hell Paul's wife was. "We'll just go inside. See what Janice is doing."

Dick stopped dead. "Janice?" he said, and lurched back around. Overhead, branches cracked and snapped against one another.

"Wait!" Paul yelled, but Dick was gone—a zombie on a mission.

So it was Janice, Paul realized as he rushed after him. *Of course*! She'd wised up, left him, and the guy had short-circuited.

Beside the leaves already, Dick held the smoldering cigar above them.

Jesus…

Paul darted forward, knocking it airborne. Ash scattered as it dropped end-over-end, sparks flying. Yelping, he stamped it into dry ground. "God damn it," he gasped. "Don't you know what you're doing?"

"Yes," Dick said. "I do."

At that moment, Paul knew, too.

Reaching from under the pile of leaves was a woman's hand—a white scar of frozen fingers against the flurry of autumn color. Cuticles were ringed with dirt, the index fingernail tacky with blood. Paul imagined what he couldn't see: Janice's stiff limbs, bruised and broken, dead mouth choked with leaves, eyes struck with terror forever.

The smell of gas was a living, heaving thing that curdled the air, churning Paul's guts.

Dick plucked the matchbook from his pocket, and a new flame flared.

"No," Paul pleaded. "You'll burn everything."

Dick's eyes caught Paul's, really seeing him for the first time. "God willing," he said, and dropped the match.

As the flames fed, Dick collapsed into the fire, and the winds came screaming through the woods.

Corn Dolly

E.J. Tett

The wicker man was burning, smoke and ash rose into the darkening sky and the fire crackled and popped. Tiny pieces of corn broke free and drifted upwards, glowing red as they rose into the air.

Jeanie moved away from the window and sat down on the bed. "It's traditional," she said. "Not at all sinister."

Her friend, Crystal, smiled. "It's not sinister," she confirmed. "It's burned in celebration of the harvest, when it's over the ashes will be spread on the fields."

Jeanie nodded. "I've never really paid much attention to the autumnal equinox before," she said. "Mabon. You know, I kinda hoped this whole pagan thing would be more about the magic and less about the tradition..." She trailed off and cleared her throat as Crystal frowned. "Sorry," she said.

Jeanie fiddled with the hem of her shirt and then peered out of the window again. The wicker man creeped her out.

"I've made you something," Crystal said, getting up and crossing the room to a bookcase. "I hope you like it."

"Presents?" Jeanie asked, smiling. "I love presents." She watched as her friend cradled something close to her chest. It looked like it was made from straw, whatever it was.

"It's a corn dolly," the girl explained, handing it over. "Made from the last sheaf of corn, the same as the wicker man. It will protect you from evil spirits."

Jeanie raised her eyebrows and tried to look suitably impressed rather than disappointed. The corn dolly didn't resemble a dolly at all. In fact it looked just like a tatty spiral of corn. "Thanks," she said, and she stood it beside her bed.

Crystal smiled widely then and there was a loud laugh from someone outside. "Good luck," she said.

"Good luck?" Jeanie repeated.

***

Jeanie opened her eyes and looked up at the stars. She was sprawled on her back in the middle of a harvested cornfield, hard stalks of the stuff jabbed into her and she frowned and sat up. "What the hell…" she muttered.

Something ran past her, she heard footsteps crushing the corn; she gasped and quickly got to her feet. "Who's there?" she demanded. "Crystal, is that you?!"

Nothing. Jeanie peered into the dark, blinking a couple of times until her eyes adjusted. "Great," she said. She turned around, trying to work out the way back to the farmhouse. Her arms hugged her waist as she started walking across the field.

A breath on the back of her neck made her freeze. "Crystal?" Jeanie whispered.

There was a laugh, quiet, Jeanie strained to hear which direction it came from. She spun around and stared into the gloom. "This isn't funny," she said.

Yes…

Jeanie felt her heart skip a beat at the voice, her arms tightened protectively around herself. "It isn't funny!" she said again, louder.

Oh, yes…

A tear trickled down her cheek and Jeanie lifted a hand to wipe it away quickly. There was a rustle to her left and she startled and turned towards the sound.

Hilarious… The voice whispered to the other side of her now and Jeanie turned sharply again.

"Crystal!" she growled, trying to sound angry and unafraid.

Jeanie… the voice replied and then it laughed loudly. A man's laugh. No, a woman's…

Both… the voice said. *Neither…*

Jeanie found that her legs finally worked and she ran; ran from the laughter though it seemed to follow her across the field. There was light ahead and she ran towards it.

The wicker man… the voice told her.

Jeanie collapsed to her knees in front of it, though it was no longer a wicker man; just a pile of glowing ash. She sobbed and with wild eyes looked all around for what was chasing her. "Please," she muttered.

Please… the voice hissed back, mocking her. *I'm free, Jeanie. Free from the wicker man, free to roam…*

"No!" Jeanie begged, scrabbling backwards as footsteps came towards her. A shadow passed in front of her and Jeanie squealed and hurried to her feet, almost managing to stand until something grabbed her by the ankles and she fell forwards, landing inches from the ash.

The embers of corn glowed in front of her eyes and Jeanie could see something there.

Don't touch it… the voice warned her and Jeanie reached, plunging her hand through heat and pulling out the corn dolly. She spun round and thrust it as if it was a crucifix towards whatever was after her.

***

The corn dolly felt strangely warm in her hand and Jeanie frowned in confusion. She was lying on the bed in the farmhouse, her brow was slick with sweat and there were tears on her cheeks.

Crystal was smiling at her. "Congratulations," she said. "You've passed."

Reaping

Darin Kennedy

Lovers of spring worship the eternal rebirth of life: the warming temperatures, the beauty of nature coming out of its cocoon, the incessant chirping of birds and insects seeking mates so that the cycle of life can start all over again.

Screw spring. Fall is real. Fall is what's coming for everyone. Rich or poor, black or white, gay or straight, American or Chinese. There comes a time when the leaves of everyone's life turn yellow, then brown, then fall to the ground. Some people call it autumn, though I think they're just dressing it up. Plus, I far prefer the term used when we were still mostly agrarian.

Harvest.

My feet crunch the yellow poplar leaves at my feet as I circle the lake. Festival At The Park is more crowded than I remember it from past years. There are the usual artists, magicians, clowns, and corn dog vendors. But lemonade costs five dollars and a plate of chicken fingers ten.

And people say I drive a hard bargain.

I keep my gloves on, though it's unseasonably warm for late September. Last thing I need is to start a panic. I just need a little bit of the stuff and I'll be good to go for another couple of weeks. I pass on a couple making out on a park bench. Ditto the mother of three with her trio of leashed devils tangling before her like some demented cat's cradle. Then I see him.

Eighty if he's a day, the old black man wears a cap that signifies his service in the Korean War. Some people who wear that kind of stuff are looking for a handout or pity.

Not this guy. He carries himself proudly, despite the cane and his uneven gait.

I approach him carefully. Don't want to spook him.

"Hello there." I motion to his hat. "Korea, eh?"

"You here for me?"

I don't know what to say. "Just saying hello."

"My daughter said you'd be here tonight. Said it was in the

cards, if you believe in that kind of stuff."

I try to figure out the inscrutable expression on his face. "Who is it you think you're talking to?"

"Death."

"Sorry, I need to keep moving." I turn to leave.

"Hey. I'm not afraid of you and you definitely shouldn't be afraid of me."

"Very well. Why are you here?"

"I didn't come for the fine cuisine, that's for sure. Grandson can eat his weight in corn dogs, but me, not so much."

"Do you… want to die?"

"Worked doing roofing for twenty-five years. Retired a few years back. Six months ago, I woke up and couldn't breathe right. All the damn asbestos left me with that mesothelioma shit you hear about in the commercials." His laugh is a long wheeze. "Class action suit back in '98 got me four hundred whole dollars. Didn't go too far, I'll tell you."

"I imagine not." His expression is unreadable. "So, you're already dying?"

"We're all dying. Me, just a little faster than the rest of you."

In all my years of doing this, I've never had a conversation like this before. I almost feel… is this guilt?

"Are you in any pain?"

He sits on a park bench and pats the space by his side.

"Let's get this over with." His earnestness surprises me.

I sit by him and pull off my gloves. Stoic as he is, he can't help but gasp. I take his hand in mine and feel his bony, arthritis-ridden knuckles.

"One thing I've got to know," he says. "Is it painless?"

Five minutes later, I rise from the bench and leave his already cooling body sitting there, staring straight ahead. I'll have to find another soon, as he was so sick that his essence will most likely only sustain me a few days. But not tonight. The breeze is cool and I think this gentleman has earned everyone else here a reprieve.

At least for tonight.

To The Devil, a Goat

Douglas J Lane

Gordie sighed and shifted his position, crunching leaves under his feet, and glared at Bobby. "This is the dumbest thing you've ever talked me into."

As if in agreement with Gordie, the goat they'd staked beside the tree bleated.

"My grandpa never lied," Bobby said. He cast a glance to the west. The lowest arc of the sun, muzzy from the thin veil of clouds, had touched the horizon. "As soon as the sun sets, he'll come out of that hole."

They'd cleared the kaleidoscope of fallen leaves to expose the hollow. It dipped deep under the old maple tree. Both tree and hole had been there as long as anyone could recall, south of town, where the roads to the four compass points crossed. It was narrow, just wide enough to accommodate a grown man if he wriggled. But even with a spider web of roots to climb down, no one explored it, not even in the summers when the pond went dry from the heat and the kids crazy from boredom. The maple was left alone. Old timers told stories.

Billy's grandpa was an old timer.

"Balls he will," Gordie said. He spat onto the dusty ground. "The devil don't live under that tree."

"No, he don't," Billy agreed. "He lives in Hell. But once a year, he comes to earth, at the moment the sun sets on the equinox, when scales tip in favor of night. He takes a sacrifice. Then he roams through the night."

"Everyone knows his night is Halloween."

Billy looked Gordie straight in the eyes, his gaze cool. "Everyone don't know anything."

The sun was halfway past the horizon. Its light washed everything pink. "What about up at the north pole, where the night goes for six months?" Gordie asked.

"No holes in the tundra," Billy said. He coiled a second length of chain around his arm. It was silver, the same as the chain that tethered the goat. The goat bleated again as if to offer advice on Billy's technique. "You can go if you're scared."

Gordie snorted and held his ground. He was the biggest of the sophomore kids and already played left tackle for the varsity football team. "And miss my chance to laugh at you?"

"You won't be laughing when we catch him," Billy said, and widened the choke chain at the end of his coil. "He's got powers. There's lots a guy can do with that."

Getting the goat had been easy enough. Old Man Hansen's stock was always wandering out of his barns. No one would miss it. It was only going to wind up slaughtered anyway. The chains had been dunked in holy water, an abuse of Billy's altar boy access to the church that he felt was justified. You couldn't catch the devil without something blessed.

Billy stood like a cowboy, feet apart, coil of chain ready. "When he goes for the goat, I'll get the loop over his head. Then you have to help me tie him good."

"Uh-huh. Soon as you lasso him."

Billy looked over his shoulder, watched the last sliver of sun as it vanished below the horizon. "Get ready!" He glanced at Gordie, but Gordie was already staring at the hole, his eyes crinkled in a squint. Billy turned.

A girl was climbing from the darkness. Billy guessed she was no older than nine or ten. There was dirt smudged on her cheeks and around her dark eyes. Her hair was matted, unwashed. Billy saw her checkered dress was tattered along the hem, snagged and torn. She was sobbing as she crawled onto the dirt and leaves from within the hollow. She looked from Gordie to Billy.

"Help me," she said. "I fell in there."

Billy set the chain aside and walked to the girl. He helped her up. She tried to straighten her soiled dress, sniffling.

"I was walking," she said, dazed, "and fell right through the leaves. I don't know when." She coughed and dirt crumbled from her hair. "I'm Lucy."

"I'm Billy. This is Gordie." Billy studied the girl. Grime was packed under her fingernails. Her hands were raw from climbing the roots out of the hole. His task forgotten, he offered the girl a smile. "It'll be okay."

"Will you walk me home?" she asked, and both boys nodded. *It was the right thing to do*, Billy thought. The girl was trembling in the twilight. She seemed to be in shock

"Sure. Where do you live?" Billy asked.

"This way," Lucy said, and offered her hands. Billy took one in his, and Gordie took the other.

As she led them towards the hollow, Billy felt as if he was forgetting something, but he couldn't recall what, even as the vise-like grip on his hand pulled him into darkness, even as his bones snapped and the mingled smells of offal and sulfur filled his nostrils. *Something*, he thought. *Something about a lasso.*

The old tree shook. Branches groaned and fell silent.

Alone, the goat bleated in the gathering dusk.

Red Sun, Autumn Rose

Eden Royce

Japan - Edo Period (Fall, 1673)

Gossip spread through the Kyoto bordello like a dry grass fire, swift and devastating. Courtesans in gaudy satins whispered to each other behind their delicate fingers as they clustered under the glowing scarlet lights of the Shimabara pleasure house.

"Did you hear about Tomiko?"

"I never trusted her."

"And with good reason."

Naomi struggled up the stone stairs, her aged bones protesting all the way to the courtesan's quarters. Her grey kimono, worn but crisp and starched, hung from her stooped frame. She slid the screen door open and followed the sound of water coming from deep inside the rooms.

"Tomiko, we must speak."

The beauty in the wooden bathtub didn't open her eyes. "What do you want? I have an important customer coming tonight. I need to ready myself." Her skin was smooth and poreless, her face a white moon floating above the steaming water.

"They are saying—"

"Who are '*they*'? The disease-ridden whores or the brainless servants?"

"They are all talking about what you did."

"I did nothing!" Tomiko rose from the hot bath, water streaming down her slender form. A servant rushed up with soft cloths to dry her, but she snatched them away. "Go get my *furisode*," she said.

Naomi followed her to the carved dressing table where the woman dried herself.

The girl returned with a lightweight kimono. Pale green dragons danced among rosy lotus blossoms on a background of ivory silk. Tomiko's eyebrows came together in a frown.

"Are you stupid? Lotus is a spring flower. The Rice Harvest Festival begins tonight. What does that mean?"

The servant trembled under her mistress's glare and whispered, "It is autumn."

"So what should I wear?"

"Chrysanthemums or maple leaves."

"Bring the maple leaves." The girl rushed off as Tomiko shook her head and opened a jar of scented cream. "I am the most popular of your night maidens. You should not let anyone speak against me. I keep you in business."

"Yes, but if you dishonor this place again by stealing another's client, I will throw you out on the streets. Without a reputable pleasure house, *you* will be the diseased whore."

"Get out!" Tomiko threw the jar at the old woman, but she ducked around the room divider. The porcelain jar smashed against the screen and the oily cream sank into the wood.

***

Tomiko rushed along the street and down a side alley, accompanied by the wooden clicks of her *geta*. She lifted the hem of the heavily decorated silk kimono to keep the filth from her costume. Her fist pummeled a cracked wooden door. "Open up!"

The warped door parted a fraction, enough to let out a dry croak. "Closed! Come back tomorrow."

"It will only take a minute." Tomiko tried to push the door wider with no result.

"No! Go away. Too late."

"I need the rose beauty cream. You make it special for me."

The door opened a hair wider. "What happen to the last one I sold you?"

"Someone stole it from my room. Probably my maid." When she wasn't welcomed in, Tomiko's temper flared. "My client tonight is Nakamura, one of the shogun's guards. If you don't sell me that cream right now, I will tell him to close down your pitiful shop."

The door opened.

***

Tomiko rubbed the scented cream into her face and neck to give her skin a pearlescent shimmer. This time, it also made her skin tingle. Perhaps the chemist rushed and added too much mint oil. She sniffed her palms, but the only scent was her trademark *hamanasu*, the autumn rose.

Rust and gold maple leaves fluttered on the bronze silk kimono as Tomiko descended the stairs toward Nakamura. Every pair of eyes in the lavish waiting area turned to her. A collective gasp filled the room. One of the other concubines fainted.

She walked up to Nakamura, but he did not bow and take her hand. He stared at her, his mouth open in shock and horror.

"What is wrong, Nakamura-san? It is not like you to forget your manners." She reached toward him and he shrank from her touch.

"Why do you all look as though you have seen a ghost?" Tomiko strode over to the mirrored glass at the entrance to the pleasure house. Her skin melted like candle wax over her skull. One eye drooped lower than the other. Her lower lip hung open like that of a suffocating fish as it gasped for breath. The thick black hair she so intricately styled began to pull away from her scalp under the weight of pearl studded combs.

As she yanked the combs free, clumps of hair and scalp came with them. She screamed and ran out into the night.

***

Naomi walked in the moonlight along the edge of the fields where harvested rice lay in bundles, undisturbed. The farmers had joined the festivities several nights ago, saying a hideous ghost now haunted the crops at night and frightened away small animals and thieves. Each morning only a few handfuls of rice were stripped from the sheaves.

Movement caught the old woman's eye. Naomi watched openmouthed as the ghost, in its tattered dress of glittering leaves, knelt among the rice bundles to gather her payment.

Harvest

Emma Kathryn

Lucy's detour through the park was not planned, but a spontaneous decision. She had just handed in her last assignment of the semester and was in a good mood. The kind of good mood that makes a girl do stupid things, like walk through the park at dusk.

Fall was her favorite time of year. Always a sucker for pretty colors, she was drawn to the dying trees, whose leaves were turning orange, then red, then brown, then falling to the ground to decay. She loved traipsing through a sea of warm hues, kicking up the crunching leaves with the toe of her boot. Slowly, the sun set behind her, darkening the path she trod through. There was nobody else passing through the park at this time. Lucy found this strange, considering that it was usually a spot popular with dog walkers. But this evening, the place was empty, save for her.

Moving even deeper into the wooded area of the park, she began to really feel the cold and wrapped her scarf tight around her body. Dark hair poked out from under her hat, tickling at her face. Irritated, she pushed it away; her good mood sinking with the sun. She shivered.

In this part of the park, the trees had lost even more leaves than those on the outskirts. They were practically mere wooden skeletons of the glorious creatures that they had once been. Almost in the heart of the spot now, Lucy suddenly felt uneasy. Glancing up, it seemed as if the aging trees were curling down towards the path. Spindly branches reached for her, begging her for help. Her heart beat a little faster. Time to hurry home.

Lucy picked up the pace, feet crunching through the thickening forest litter on the ground below her. Here, the leaves were practically dust; dust which clung to her boots and the edges of her jeans. The crunching was the only sound to be heard. Moving faster and faster, she was tempted to break into a run. Only her common sense stopped her from doing so, telling herself that trees couldn't harm her.

That is, until she came to one sitting directly in the middle of the path. She stopped moving. Unable to believe what she was seeing, Lucy glanced around. She wasn't quite sure why. Surely, nobody could move a tree as some kind of elaborate prank. Taking a brave step forward, she discovered that the structure was fixed firmly in the ground, with a single root erupting from the soil, sticking out at a peculiar angle. Lucy took another step. Why hadn't she seen this tree until now? Why hadn't she noticed it as she had approached? On closer study, she could see that this tree only held a couple of scarlet leaves. Its time was almost over for this year. Approaching still, Lucy examined the bark, which looked brittle and coarse. Some tiny voice in her head told her to touch it and she did.

But the bark was not brittle at all. Lucy gasped in horror as her fingers did not touch wood, but slid through something sticky instead. Quickly, she pulled her hand away, but the goo went with her, clinging to her fingers. It seemed like sap, but she had never seen any tree like this before. The stuff would not come off her skin. Stupidly, she tried to wipe it away with her other hand, but the substance simply started to spread to both hands. Lucy screamed, but the rest of the park was empty. No one heard her. The sticky material began to travel up her arms and pull her towards the tree. Fighting pointlessly, Lucy was dragged against her will until she was up against the trunk of the tree, which also gave way to her touch. Arms were now gone, soaked up inside the tree, as too were parts of her legs. Lucy screamed again, her head held back in an attempt to stay above the surface of the substance. But it was no use. Mid-scream, the tree sucked her in entirely, swallowing her whole.

The park was silent once more and the tree in the center of the path suddenly burst into bloom again, its dying branches filled with lush, green leaves. Now stocked with a harvest of youthful energy, this tree was one of the few whose beauty would make it through the coming winter, unscathed.

Turkey Shoot

Hal Kempka

The snowstorm hit without warning after Carrie and Bart had driven midway across the southern Minnesota prairie. Drifting snow and black ice clogged the highways and slowed traffic. In no time, the four-hour trek along the two lane highway to visit his family for Thanksgiving became a nightmare.

A bitter wind buffeted the car as they drove through a thick stand of barren elms, oaks, and maples. Up ahead, three abandoned cars and a jack-knifed big rig clogged the ditches on either side of the road. They were the first vehicles the couple had seen in twenty miles.

"There must be black ice," Bart said, slowing the car to a crawl.

The snow tires lost their grip periodically, sending the car drifting aimlessly across the icy patches until they caught dry asphalt. Carrie craned her neck, scanning the accident scene. Several windows were shattered and blood stained the doors.

"My God, this looks like something out of a horror movie. Did you see all the blood?"

"Yeah, I guess we'll have to be extra careful."

Carrie shivered. "What's eerie is there aren't any people."

"The state police probably transported them to hospitals and hotels."

At that moment, two wild turkeys flew directly in front of them, gobbling loud enough to be heard inside the car. They awkwardly flapped their wings and barely avoided hitting the windshield. Carrie thought one turkey, that clipped its tail feathers on the side view mirror, had flashed an angry glance.

"Whoa!" Bart said. "Did you see the size of those birds? They were almost as big as a man. If I had my shotgun, we'd be bagging a fresh turkey to take to the family. Just like the pioneer days."

"Yeah, right," Carrie shot back. "Some pioneers we'd make. We're driving a Land Rover, and our idea of roughing it is checking into a lousy three-star hotel and buying lunch at a drive-through."

Dusk set in, and the barren trees cast ominous shadows across the road. They passed another car that sheared off a road sign. The grill and front bumper were deeply creased, and the sign had speared the windshield. More patches of blood soaked the snow, and holes riddled the side windows.

"Bart, I'm not kidding; this is getting scary," Carrie said, her voice cracking. "Maybe we should turn around and go back home."

"Nah, we've got snow tires and four-wheel drive. As long as we take it slow and easy, we'll be fine. Some hunters probably were shooting at a pheasant and errant pellets hit the car.

"You think we should call your family? They might be worried."

"Yeah," Bart said, handing Carrie his cell phone. "Call them and tell them we'll probably arrive late tonight because of the storm."

She punched the numbers, but the 'call failed' light kept appearing on the phone screen.

"No signal," Carrie said.

They heard a muffled gunshot and another turkey flew across the road.

"There must still be a couple of hunters out," Bart said. "I hope they don't mistake us for a turkey."

"That's not funny," Carrie replied.

She no more than finished the sentence when another shot peppered the Land Rover with pellets.

"Son of a bitch!" Bart hollered. "Hang on!"

He accelerated sharply, but the car hit more black ice. As the car spun to the right, Bart steered into the spin. He eased up on the accelerator, trying to regain control while the car fish-tailed down the highway.

A third shot punched a huge hole in the driver's side windshield. Carrie screamed as the top of Bart's head exploded like a melon.

Gray matter and blood splattered the headliner and back seat. Bubbles gurgled from his mouth as he slumped forward on the steering wheel.

The car spun out of control and broadsided a road sign. Carrie shielded her face with her arms, screaming hysterically. Her head slammed against the passenger window, knocking her unconscious.

She awoke lying outside the car in the snow and tried to roll over. Her arms and legs however, felt numb, and she couldn't move. The air smelled curiously of blood and wet feathers.

Carrie's face felt warm and sticky and blood trickled into her eyes, blurring her vision. She sensed someone standing over her and blinked her eyelids to clear away the coagulating blood. After finally forcing them open, she screamed and passed out.

An enormous wild turkey stood over her cradling a shotgun beneath one wing. It cocked its head and stared down at her with dark, rapidly blinking eyes. Its pale pink waddle shook and a sinister smile slowly curled across its beak.

"I think we've bagged our limit, don't you think?"

Another turkey standing beside it emitted a throaty gobble.

"Yeah. Put the human out of her misery and let's go. Now that we've bagged our limit, we have enough meat to feed the entire flock."

Another shot rang out, and a trail of blood stained the snow as the turkeys dragged Bart and Carrie off into the night.

Little Toads

Sean Logan

"Mr. Branson!"

Albert Branson rubbed his temples. The fat child's voice was like an ice pick in his ears.

"Yes, Rory?"

"I have to go to the bathroom."

"Well, you'll just have to go in your pants."

Rory's fat, freckled face turned a bright shade of red. The class giggled. Little blond Robbie stuck his finger in Rory's face and laughed. Every titter was as grating as an alarm clock to Albert.

Not even a month into the fall semester and already this was his worst class ever. Albert thought that every year, but seriously, this was the worst.

"Okay, everybody sit down and shut up; we're going to watch a movie."

The class stopped giggling. There was a dull throbbing in the back of Albert's head.

Rory shook off his embarrassment and went back to being annoying. "Mr. Branson! Did you know Mr. Kostyal-Lampathakis?"

Albert took a big drink of cold, stale coffee.

"Who's Mr. Kampa... who's that?"

"He was our old teacher. He wore a gray hat with a flower on it."

"No, I never met him."

"He died."

Albert didn't know that. All he knew was a full-time gig had opened up in the middle of nowhere; and that was fine with him. He'd been looking all summer and found that he was unemployable anywhere decent.

"Oh, yeah?" Albert said.

"He died of poison."

"Okay, great. Now clam up, we're gonna watch..." What did he have here? Dirty Dancing. Found it on the book shelf in the teachers' lounge. "We're going to see a dancing movie."

"Did you know we have poison frogs around these parts? They're yellow and they have black spots. And red eyes."

Albert stuck the video tape into a top-loading VCR from a long-gone era.

"People lick them," said a skinny kid. Albert didn't know his name. He wore glasses so thick they made his eyes look like raisins.

"What?" Albert said.

Rory jumped back in, "Yeah, some kids lick the poison frogs 'cause it's like drugs. They get all weird and see stuff and some of them died 'cause it was poison."

"Mr. Branson!" skinny yelled. "Does that mean Mr. Kostyal-Lampathakis was licking frogs?"

"I doubt it. Most people stop being that stupid when they stop being kids. But then again, I've met some of your parents. Now shut it, I'm going to start the movie."

Albert pressed play and shut off the lights. He fell into his seat and took another drink of horrible coffee. Last night had his head in vice. He went to the neighborhood dive hoping to bring back one of the local hillbilly chicks but came home with nothing but a head full of Jim Beam.

"Mr. Branson!" Rory bellowed.

"Shut it, Rory, the movie's starting."

"I just wanted to tell you that when they found Mr. Kostyal-Lampathakis, he had red foam coming out of his mouth."

"I SAID SHUT THE FUCK UP!"

Rory jerked back in his seat. His stunned look slowly balled up into red-faced frustration. It wasn't the first time Albert had snapped at him but the kid was seriously pressing his buttons. Albert was practically a saint for how he was dealing with that brat.Last time a kid pressed his buttons like that it didn't end so well—for the brat or himself. One got a dislocated shoulder and the other got disciplinary action, a loss of tenure and a job in Bumfuck, Nowhere.

"Just watch the movie," Albert said. "I'm going to rest my eyes a little."

His head felt worse now, the yelling making his temples throb. And he was sweating. It was as hot out as mid-summer, only twice as humid.

Albert swallowed a big, cold mouthful of coffee, hoping the caffeine would make the headache go away.

He closed his eyes but his head continued spinning and feverish colors swirled under his eyelids. He opened his eyes to find Rory staring at him, his fat arms folded, the dancing light of the TV throwing shifting shadows across his face.

Albert was not feeling well at all, his stomach started to twist into a painful knot. This hangover was just more than he could handle. Someone was going to have to take over.

He pushed himself up out of his chair and the whole room seemed to swim up around him, his head spinning, stomach lurching. He flopped back into his seat and the room came splashing down with him.

The rest of the class was starting to turn slowly toward him.

Rory was smiling, his arms still folded. The light from the TV kept his eyes in shadow.

All of the kids were staring at Albert now, some giggling, little blond Robbie was pointing at him and laughing in slow motion.

Sweat was pouring down Albert's face. His throat was dry and closing up. He needed a drink, reached out for his coffee, but the muscles in his arms were cramping tight.

"Mr. Branson," Rory said, rising to his feet.

Albert got his fingers around the coffee mug and brought it to his mouth. He could feel his throat closing. He tilted the cup, and with the cold, foul-tasting coffee, something solid slid against his lips.

Rory walked around Albert's desk to the front of the class.

The room seemed to shift suddenly and Albert slipped to the floor, his arms and legs twitching.

"Mr. Branson," Rory said, staring down at him, "Mr. Kostyal-Lampathakis told me to shut up once."

With a foamy copper taste in his mouth, Albert noticed the three small, yellow creatures, covered in black spots that had slid out of his coffee mug. But he only saw them for a moment as the bending, twisting room grew dark around him.

Paradise Road

Kathee Jantzi

Nicky's white knuckles gripped the steering wheel at a proper ten and two. She tried to relax her grip. "I know we don't talk much at school, but I invited you out tonight because I need your help."

"I can't help you," Tracey answered. She wore black from head-to-toe, complete with thick eyeliner. She drummed her nails on the car's dashboard.

Nicky took a left on Paradise Road. "Erin's still there. I know it."

The full moon seemed to be lighting her way to the quarter mile haunted stretch of Paradise Road outside of the small town of Jefferson, Wisconsin, where everyone knew the rules: never stop the car, never get out of the car, and never go into the woods on the left hand side. Two nights ago, Nicky disobeyed the rules and now her best friend was missing. They got separated and no one had seen or heard from her since. Nicky had heard her chilling scream and called 9-1-1. Today, authorities had called off the search. But Nicky wouldn't give up. She took a deep breath and lifted one hand off the steering wheel, flipping it over to stare at it. She couldn't see it shaking but ever neuron in her body told her she was quivering on the inside.

"Let the police find her," Tracey said.

"They've given up," Nicky snapped.

The haunted section of the road was marked by a canopy of overhanging oak trees and spray painted signs reading: *Keep Off* and *Danger*. Nicky felt the air thicken and the temperature drop. She slowed the car to a crawl. Fog swirled on the road and a stiff autumn wind tossed the dead leaves. Slivers of pale moonlight made shadows on the road.

"Can't you help? Everyone knows you have that sixth sense thing," Nicky could feel her heartbeat in her throat and her hand tremor became visible.

Tracey rolled up her window. "It's not safe in there for you and I'm sorry to be the one to tell you this, but Erin is gone."

"No, she's not!" Nicky caught the sight of something rustling in the underbrush. She slammed on her brakes as a creature skittered into the middle of the road.

A raccoon. Without a head.

The animal stopped and twisted its neck in their direction, fresh blood spurting from a severed artery but leaving no trace on the road.

"That's her!" Nicky slammed the car in park and whipped open her door.

Tracey grabbed her arm. "Last warning. Don't get out of the car."

Untangling herself, Nicky left the vehicle and pursued the raccoon on foot. The weight of the woods seemed to push on her lungs and she gulped to get more air. The evening fog smothered her from every direction. She smelled damp leaves, mold, and rotting despair. Branches broke in the direction of the creature's disappearance. She sped up and found old tire tracks of mud. She quickened her pace, moving deeper and deeper into the abyss. Every time she heard a noise, her heart stopped.

"Erin!" she shouted. She glimpsed the raccoon under a tree and then it vanished. The tire tracks ended and she stood under a towering oak with a ladder leaning up against it. Her eyes drifted upwards. Five tattered nooses were tied to a long branch.

Behind her, leaves rustled and a branch cracked. "Who's there?" She spun around. Tracey seemed to materialize out of the fog. Nicky let out of a sigh. "I think I found something. That raccoon disappeared right here and look," she said, gesturing to the ropes. "Do you think people have committed suicide here?"

"No," Tracey said. "They were hung."

A violent wave of nausea hit Nicky. She doubled over and clung to the trunk of the tree with one hand while she puked. Beads of cold sweat dotted her forehead. "What the hell happened here?"

Tracey's eyes glazed over as she stared at the nooses. "My people were murdered here by locals. During a ritual." She smiled at Nicky. "The entire coven. Hung by your ancestors. And Erin's."

In a flash, Tracey saw the pentagram, heard the witches' incantations and inhaled the incense. Then the locals emerged, bundles of rope heavy in their hands. The women screamed and cursed while they were bound and the nooses affixed. Their necks snapped in succession and the silence of death took up residence in the woods with their trapped spirits.

Nicky held her hands up and backed away. "I didn't know. How could I know?" She hit something solid behind her. A cloaked and hooded figure hissed, "*Ssshe's one of ttthem.*"

Nicky screamed.

"She's yours," Tracey said.

Four more figures appeared on the tire tracks from the pentagram's other corners. The beings advanced. "Tracey, you have to help me!"

"*Ssshe's one of ttthem*," they repeated.

Nicky ran, trying to break between two of the beings. But a sharp pain like a jagged pitchfork hammered into her back. She screamed and arched her head back as another set of claws swiped her back and ripped through her shirt to her skin. They were on top of her and dragged her to the base of the tree. She could see Tracey's boots, then everything went black.

Blind and crawling on all fours, panic sliced through her bones.

"Nicky," she heard Erin's voice. "Is that you?"

* * *

Tracey shoved her icy hands in the pockets of her pants as she retraced her steps to Nicky's car. She collapsed in the driver's seat and swallowed the bile in her mouth before she floored the vehicle only to immediately hit the brakes.

Two decapitated raccoons emerged from the left hand side of the road. They craned their headless necks in her direction.

Her Wiccan ancestors wanted revenge.

And what her ancestor's wanted, Tracey knew better than to refuse.

Problem Solving Beneath the Harvest Moon

Adrian Ludens

Eubank leaned on his shovel and peered across the empty field at the squat buildings that comprised his poultry farm. The bloated Harvest Moon hung in the sky like a giant leering jack-o-lantern and Eubank suddenly wished for cloud cover. In years past, Eubank had used the light brought on by the moon's strong fall presence to work longer into the night, reaping the rewards of his spring and summer labors. But too much heat and too little rain for too many seasons had forced the farmer to adapt or die.

Eubank remembered how the hope and terror had intermingled on his wife's face as he told her about the bank loan. He converted his operation to a chicken farm. Eubank spat in the dirt and scowled. Lord, how they stank. Now, his fields were all left fallow and his every effort went into increasing poultry production.

Not that he was a greedy man; though deep in debt, Eubank still paid his migrant workers close to a living wage. He wanted to do more, but the system wouldn't let him. What could he do? Eubank shrugged under the scrutiny of the moon. A chilly October breeze tugged at his flannel shirt as if to remind him he had work to complete. Eubank sighed and sank the shovel blade deep into the cool earth. As the hole slowly grew like a pool of spilled ink, the chicken farmer considered his problems one by one.

The environmental and animal cruelty groups endlessly crusaded against him. Eubank knew his operation created mountains of waste, polluted ground water, and posed health hazards for his workers. If someone showed him a better way, he'd be happy to adopt it. Until then, there was nothing he could do but keep working with what he had available.

Eubank had started to worry about another growing threat. The news reports called it 'rural commodity theft.' Times were so tough that city folks were sneaking out to farms and ranches, stealing everything from gasoline to timber; crops to livestock. Now farmers had to protect themselves against those they worked to feed?

Eubank shook his head and spat again in disgust. He shoveled dirt for a few minutes more. With so many problems facing him, this time alone helped Eubank keep everything in perspective. But tonight, the odor of the freshly turned soil and the trickle of sweat down his back somehow made him feel melancholy. Eubank wished he had all the answers in these hard times.

Then, to add to his worries, last night Eubank had caught the new guy on the crew in bed with his teenage daughter Lana. Eubank had heard Miguel and Esteban calling the newcomer 'Romeo' in days prior. Eubank now wondered if that had truly been his name. He would not tolerate this kind of behavior. One couldn't allow a migrant worker—and an illegal, no doubt—to take these kinds of liberties. Next, the inmates would be running the asylum.

Eubank scowled at the leering moon and tossed his shovel aside. He walked back to the bed of the pickup and dropped the rusty, battered tailgate.

Eubank grunted as he dragged Romeo's body through the dirt toward the freshly dug hole. Here, at least, was one problem he knew how to solve.

The Hiding Place

R. Maguire

I did it again on Saturday. So in the twilight hours of Sunday, they buried me.

"Remember, this isn't a punishment," mom said. She said that every time it happened. "It's for protection, so no one finds you. We love you, no matter what."

Dad, drenched in sweat despite the cool autumn breeze, nodded in agreement.

Upset I stepped into the five-foot coffin, with only a pillow, a gallon of water, bottle of pills and a few granola bars.

"If you feel scared, take one of those pills. They'll relax you enough to sleep." Then they closed the lid despite my sobs and lowered me into the ground.

The only imperfection in the expensive box was a hole that dad had drilled at the top. He attached a large piece of tubing through the hole and sealed the edges to prevent water and dirt from entering. The oversized hose ran up from my box, through the ground and terminated just above the surface. The large hose provided fresh air and when I was lucky a candy bar or two would slide down it to let me know that my parents were still there.

Two years after the first '*accident*,' my nine-year-old body still fit comfortably in the box. I had returned to this shallow grave on six occasions in that time span. I wasn't as terrified now compared to the first few times I had been hidden. I learned to embrace the quiet darkness. The problem was the cold. Now that fall had arrived the weather was starting to cool and it was even colder underground. But, as mother said, it was necessary so others wouldn't try to take me away for what I had done.

***

Of all the times I'd been buried, this one felt different. I usually hid for three or four days. Today, if it *was* daytime, seemed more like five or six days. I had taken more pills than ever before so it was possible my count was off. However, there had been no candy deliveries so far, no fruit skins dropped to improve the smell, and nothing to let me know my parents were still around. The box reeked from where I soiled it. And the quiet, black nothingness continued.

I popped another pill to calm my growing concern. Fifteen minutes would bring woozy carelessness but until then I would have to suffer my thoughts.

Had my parents finally given up on me? Would this become my true grave? I had promised to stop in the past. I told them I'd be a good boy, but the urges kept returning. It happened less and less, but still, eight '*accidents*,' as mom called them, was a lot in two years. Perhaps they no longer loved me and this is how it would end.

Light tears rolled down my cheek. My heart rate doubled and breathing intensified. I downed another pill.

I knew I was different. We rarely spoke about it, but I knew other children did not act as I did. I didn't choose to be different, but I was. I usually succeeded at being a normal child, and it was fun. But in the end, desire always got the best of me. Playing with fake toys and climbing trees was not as fun as playing with dead things.

I didn't mean to hurt little Suzie Bell. Her tiny skull was fragiler than I thought; but I can be a good boy from now on, I vowed in my head. At this point I would do anything to rid myself of another horrid second in the cold, wet box.

They don't love me anymore. They're tired of their monster son. In a voice so low I barely heard it, I promised, " If I get out of here and they forgive me, I'll never kill another—"

I stopped; something descended the hose and plopped onto the pine floor. I felt around for the delivery, careful not to touch spots that I had soiled. My fingers finally came to rest on top of a bar. I brought it up to my face and unwrapped the plastic. The chocolate peanut butter erased the rancid smells of earlier and I smiled in the darkness.

The candy gesture was so small and yet because of it I knew everything would be fine. They still loved me. Mommy and Daddy still loved their little monster. They must just need more time to make things right. I leaned back against the soft pillow, the grin never leaving my lips as I ate the candy bar.

Finally at ease, I tried to remember what I was thinking about just before my treat had arrived. The pills were working now and I hadn't a clue as to what I was saying earlier. Oh well, it couldn't have been that important.

I stared into the darkness and thought about all the things I would do when it was safe for me to come up from the ground again.

www.ingramcontent.com/pod-product-compliance
Lightning Source LLC
LaVergne TN
LVHW090939080826
845145LV00003B/809

* 9 7 8 0 9 8 4 5 4 0 8 2 2 *